"You g_____ ___ _____
your _n_____ _____
so dan_____ _____

I glanced at Joe. "No, w_____ _____
cycles," I said. Of course, I didn't telling her we were riding *Jet Skis*.

Belinda was starting to ask another question when her brother came running out of the house, shaking his fists.

"Everything's gone!" he shouted.

Belinda looked at him and sighed. "What's gone, Brian?"

"The stereo! The TV! The computer!" he yelled.

Belinda looked confused. "What are you talking about?"

"Someone must have broken in after we evacuated," said Brian.

"You mean . . . ?"

"Yes! We've been robbed!"

THE HARDY BOYS

UNDERCOVER BROTHERS™

Available from Simon & Schuster

THE HARDY BOYS

BOYS

UNDERCOVER BROTHERS™

#11 Hurricane Joe

FRANKLIN W. DIXON

Aladdin Paperbacks
New York   London   Toronto   Sydney

First Aladdin Paperbacks edition August 2006
Copyright © 2006 by Simon & Schuster, Inc.

☙ ALADDIN PAPERBACKS
An imprint of Simon & Schuster
Children's Publishing Division
1230 Avenue of the Americas
New York, NY 10020

All rights reserved, including the right of
reproduction in whole or in part in any form.
Designed by Lisa Vega
The text of this book was set in Aldine 401BT.
Printed in the United States of America
10 9 8 7 6 5 4 3

THE HARDY BOYS MYSTERY STORIES and HARDY BOYS
UNDERCOVER BROTHERS are trademarks of Simon & Schuster, Inc.
ALADDIN PAPERBACKS and colophon are trademarks of
Simon & Schuster, Inc.
Library of Congress Control Number: 2006925023

ISBN-13: 978-1-4169-1174-6
ISBN-10: 1-4169-1174-X

TABLE OF CONTENTS

1.

Slam Dunk

Question: What's worse than getting caught spying on a pair of wanted criminals?

Answer: Getting caught riding Jet Skis in the middle of a hurricane.

I should know. *Both* of them happened to me—*on the same day*, believe it or not. I'm Joe Hardy, undercover agent for American Teens Against Crime. And this is just the beginning of the most *disastrous* mission my brother Frank and I ever encountered.

Fasten your seat belts.

It's going to be a wild ride.

"Look! It's those boys!"

The deep voice bellowed like a foghorn on the deck of the freighter.

"Get 'em!"

Frank and I glanced up from our Jet Skis, shielding our eyes in the heavy rain. Above us, leaning over the side of the ship, was a tall beefy man with a short red beard, glaring down at us.

"Hi, Mr. Plotnik," I said. "We seem to be lost. Could you point us in the direction of Bayport?"

He growled at me.

Then a younger red-haired man rushed up to the railing and peeked over the side. "It's those guys from the dock, Dad," he said, slightly confused. "How did they get out here? We're miles offshore."

"They must have followed us."

"Do they need a lift?"

The beefy man grabbed his son by the shoulders. "*No!*" he roared. "They need to be liquidated!"

"What do you mean?"

"They followed us! They saw us dumping toxic waste!"

"So?"

"So they might tell the police. Do you want to go to jail?"

"No."

"Then you have to make sure they don't talk. Now get moving!"

The younger man sighed and started climbing over the railing. "Okay, okay. I'm moving. Are you happy?"

"Not until those boys are snooping on the bottom of the ocean."

While the father and son bickered, Frank and I revved up our Jet Skis to make our getaway. But just before taking off, Frank raised his camera and pointed it at the Plotniks.

"Say 'cheese.'"

He snapped a picture—and blinded them with the flash.

"Hey!" the son yelled, covering his eyes.

Way to go, Frank.

Plotnik's son was totally stunned.

Now's our chance.

I spun my Jet Ski toward the shore and sped away as fast as I could.

But Frank wasn't so lucky. Just as he started to pull away, the younger Plotnik sprang and dove off the side of the ship.

SLAM!

He knocked my brother off his Jet Ski.

DUNK!

The two of them plunged into the ocean.

"Frank!" I shouted, the wind catching in my throat.

3

I spun around and tried to circle back to help my brother. But the hurricane was gathering force, and with all the heavy rain, I couldn't see a thing.

Where did they go?

I scanned the area back and forth, my heart sinking fast.

"Frank!" I shouted again.

It was no use. My brother and his attacker were nowhere in sight.

The ocean had swallowed them up.

Okay, it's confession time. This mission of ours had turned into a total disaster, and there was only one person to blame: me.

Furthermore, I'll even state—for the record—something that I've never, ever admitted before:

I, Joe Hardy, should have listened to my brother.

Yes, you heard me. I should have listened to Frank when he said we should postpone the mission—at least until the storm blew over. I should have listened when he gave me the latest report from the Weather Network.

"It looks like Hurricane Herman is heading north," he explained. "Things could get ugly."

"Only if you look in the mirror," I joked.

"I'm serious, Joe. We don't want to get stuck in a hurricane."

"Oh, come on," I said. "A little rain won't kill us. And besides, we'll be done before the storm hits."

It seemed like a good argument. I mean, this was the kind of job Frank and I could do in our sleep. Our mission: Follow the freighter on our Jet Skis, snap pictures of those creeps dumping toxic waste, and then head back to shore. No sweat. Even the suspects—Bob and Peter Plotnik, owners of Plotnik Plastics—didn't seem like the dangerous type.

Boy, was I wrong.

"Come on, Frank," I said. "It's a slam-dunk mission."

Of course, I had no way of knowing that Frank would end up getting slammed *and* dunked.

"We've got to stop these guys," I continued. "They're human garbage. They're ruining the beaches with all that junk they dump."

"Okay, Joe," he said, finally relenting. "Let's go take out the trash."

From that moment on, everything started going wrong. And I mean *everything*.

First, the Plotniks spotted us at the Bayport docks. "Are you sure you boys want to go riding

Jet Skis?" Mr. Plotnik asked us. "There's a hurricane heading our way." We told him we'd be fine, then ducked out of sight while he and his son loaded barrels of toxic waste onto the freighter.

Twenty minutes later Frank and I followed the ship out of the bay—and were almost knocked off our Jet Skis. The waves kept getting rougher and rougher, and soon it started raining—hard. We were almost ready to turn back when the Plotniks started hauling the barrels overboard. One of them almost crushed my Jet Ski.

Then, just when I thought things couldn't get any worse, Frank fumbled for his camera—and accidentally set off the flash.

"What was that?" said a voice on the deck of the freighter.

And *that* was how the Hardy boys got caught.

That was also how I ended up riding a Jet Ski in the middle of a hurricane, wondering if I'd ever see my brother again.

"Frank!"

The storm raged around me, tossing my Jet Ski up and down, side to side, like a tiny rubber duck in a very big bathtub. The waves swelled and rolled and crashed around me. The rain was so heavy I could barely make out the dark shape of the freighter, even though it was just fifty feet away.

"Frank!"

I made my way closer to the ship. Something caught my eye—something floating and bumping against the side of the freighter.

It was Frank's Jet Ski—without Frank.

Okay, bro. Where are you?

"Frank!"

I tried to shout above the sound of the wind, but the roar of the storm drowned me out. Wiping the rain from my eyes, I glanced around until I spotted a flash of red rising up on a nearby swell.

There he was—Plotnik's red-haired son—fighting the waves.

No, wait.

He wasn't fighting the waves as much as he was fighting my *brother*. The two of them were locked in battle, arms and legs thrashing in the water.

"Frank! Hold on!"

I spun my Jet Ski around and gunned it. Up and over the crest of a massive wave, I zoomed as fast as I could toward Frank and Peter Plotnik. The big redhead was shoving my brother under the water, holding him down with both hands.

"Heads up, Red!" I shouted.

Tilting and swerving the Jet Ski, I stuck out my foot—and clobbered him good.

7

"*Ooof!*"

Peter reeled back, losing his grip on my brother. A second later Frank popped out of the water, gasping for air. I pulled up next to him and reached out my hand.

"Frank! Climb aboard!"

My brother grabbed hold and tried to pull himself up. But when he swung his leg up onto the seat, the Jet Ski dipped to the side—and almost flipped us into the ocean.

"Whoa! Steady, boy." I leaned hard to the right to counterbalance the weight.

Finally the Jet Ski stopped teetering. Frank straightened himself up and wrapped his arms around my chest. "Okay, I'm on. Let's go, bro."

I started to take off when I heard a loud shout from the freighter.

"Don't worry, Peter! I'll save you!"

I turned to see the redhead's father, Bob Plotnik, grab a life preserver and leap over the side of the ship.

Ker-sploosh!

He did a cannonball right next to his son, causing a mini tidal wave that sent the boy sailing backward.

Whap!

Peter banged his head on Frank's abandoned Jet Ski. His father swam over and helped him climb onto the seat. Then, pulling himself up, Bob Plotnik grabbed the controls and revved up the craft.

"They're coming after us, Joe," said Frank. "Move it!"

He tightened his grip as I gave it the gas, trying to steer the Jet Ski onto a wave for extra momentum.

"Hurry! They're gaining on us!"

I glanced over my shoulder. Frank was right. The Plotniks were only fifteen feet behind us.

"Joe! Look out!"

I turned my head—and gulped.

Whoosh!

A massive wave crashed into the nose of the Jet Ski. I tried to pivot and ride the swell like a champion surfer, but the force of the water knocked us into a tailspin.

I hit the gas hard and tried to regain control.

That's when the engine stalled.

"I don't believe this," I muttered, reaching for the starter. "What next?"

"Joe! Look out!" Frank yelled in my ear.

I glanced up to see Bob and Peter Plotnik zooming right toward us, like a pair of knights in a jousting competition. But instead of a long steel lance, Mr. Plotnik used his life preserver as a weapon.

Whack!

He clubbed me in the head with the round foam tube as their Jet Ski zipped past us. Stunned by the blow, I slumped down over the controls and miraculously triggered the starter.

"Stay down, Joe." Frank reached over me to steer. "Just hit the gas."

Still a little dazed, I fumbled for the accelerator and pressed down. The Jet Ski roared to life, and soon we were riding the waves, rising up in the air and slamming down hard with each splashy landing.

"*Ouch! Ouch! Ouch!*" I grunted on the bumps, my face bouncing off the dashboard. "Let me drive, Frank!"

"If you insist."

He leaned back so I could sit up. The Plotniks were heading right for us again—but this time I was ready for them. Waiting until they were about ten feet away, I swerved to the right and doused their Jet Ski with a huge spray of water.

SPLASH!

They spun out of control as I headed for the shoreline. Frank squeezed my arm. "Good job, Joe. But drive back toward the freighter."

"Why?"

"Look over there."

I gazed back at the ship. Just behind it, another boat was zooming our way. It was small, about forty-five feet long, and white with flashing lights.

"It's the U.S. Coast Guard!" I shouted.

"Yeah. See if you can lead the Plotniks right into their path."

Looking back, I waited for Bob and Peter to catch up to us, then set a course toward the freighter. Zooming around the starboard side, I figured our pursuers wouldn't spot the Coast Guard boat until it was too late.

"Here they come, Joe!"

Vrrrooom!

The waves churned and rolled as the Plotniks chased us along the side of the freighter. Leaning hard, we circled around the stern of the ship and turned onto the port side.

"And here she comes," said Frank, nodding toward the Coast Guard boat.

The small craft was fifty feet away, heading right for the Plotniks' freighter—probably to see why it was drifting during a hurricane. I slowed the Jet Ski to a stop and turned around.

"Check it out," said Frank.

The Plotniks rounded the freighter. The Coast

11

Guard boat closed in and blocked their course. We couldn't see what happened next. But we could hear Peter Plotnik yell, "Look out, Dad!" and a loud crash.

"Ouch," I muttered.

Seconds later the Coast Guard pulled Bob and Peter Plotnik out of the water. One of the officers pointed to their freighter and started asking questions.

"I think their dumping days are over," I said.

Frank tugged my arm. "Let's go see if we can hitch a ride—unless you want to navigate these killer waves all the way back to shore."

"Good idea."

I revved the engine and headed for the Coast Guard boat. Frank started waving his arm and yelling. "Over here! Help!"

But I guess they didn't see us—because the boat started speeding away.

Great.

"Hey! Wait for us!" I yelled, trying to catch up.

It was no use. The Coast Guard boat zoomed off and vanished into the rain.

"I don't believe this," I groaned.

"Just drive, Joe," said Frank. "We have to get back to the dock before this storm gets any worse."

"Worse?" I shouted. "How could this possibly get any worse?"

Mother Nature answered my question a few seconds later—with a giant twenty-foot wall of water. Rising up like a sea monster from the ocean depths, the wave lunged and curled over our heads.

Then, with a deafening roar, it came crashing down—and knocked us off our Jet Ski.

2.

Wipeout!

WHOOMP!

The wave hit us full force, plunging us deeper and deeper into the churning water. I tightened my grip around my brother's waist—but the ocean was a lot stronger than I was. The current tore us apart with a sharp jolt, tossing us in opposite directions. Tumbling and spinning, I couldn't even tell which way was up.

Now I know what it feels like to be a gym sock in a washing machine.

When the "spin cycle" was finally over, I tried to swim for the surface. My lungs screamed for air, and I didn't know how much longer I could stay under.

You can do it, Frank, I told myself.

Finally I reached the surface, gasping for air.

"Joe!" I shouted.

No response.

"JOE!"

Nothing—except the sounds of the wind and the waves.

I shouted again, then waited. And waited. Finally, a voice answered me.

"Frank! Over here!"

I spun around in the water. My brother was about forty feet away, bobbing up and down in the waves.

"Hey! What's up, bro?" I yelled.

"Nothing much!" he shouted back. "What's up with you?"

"Nothing. Just hanging."

We started swimming toward each other when—*BANG*—something hit me in the head.

It was our Jet Ski, floating upside down in the water. I rubbed my head, then grabbed onto one of the skis and held on tight. Joe swam up next to me and reached for the other ski.

"We're alive," he said, panting.

"Yeah," I replied. "Let's try to keep it that way."

"Do you think this thing still works?" he asked, nodding at the Jet Ski.

15

I shrugged. "The engine's probably flooded. But it's worth a try."

"Okay, let's flip it over," Joe said, bracing his hands on the edge of the Jet Ski. "On the count of three. One. Two. Three!"

We pushed up as hard as we could, kicking our feet and lunging forward until the Jet Ski rolled right side up. I helped Joe climb onto the seat. Then he leaned over and pulled me up. Straddling the seat behind him, I wrapped my arms around his chest.

"Okay, I'm ready," I said. "Start her up."

"Keep your fingers crossed." Joe reached for the ignition and turned the key.

The engine coughed a few times—and died.

"Try it again," I said.

He tried it again.

Same thing. Just a few coughs and then—nothing.

"Now what?" said Joe.

"I guess we just sit here and hope the waves will carry us back to shore."

"But what if they carry us out to sea?"

"Maybe a ship will spot us and save us."

"But what if a ship doesn't spot us? What if we run into a bunch of hungry sharks instead?"

"They'd probably take one bite and spit you

out, Joe. All that hair product you use—*yuck*."

"I'm serious, Frank."

I sighed. "Don't worry. We're going to get out this. We always do, don't we? You and I have been on dozens of missions, and we haven't been killed yet."

"There's a first time for everything, Frank."

I gave up. "Okay, have it your way. We're going to die out here. We're going to drift out to sea and get eaten by sharks. Are you happy now?"

"Very."

"Really?"

"Yeah."

Mr. Plotnik must have done some serious damage when he hit my brother with the life preserver. "Why are you happy, Joe?" I asked.

"Because I can see Bayport," he said, pointing. "Look. Over there."

I squinted my eyes. The rain was easing up, and I could just make out the rooftops of our hometown. I instantly recognized the city hall and church steeple rising above the town square.

"That's Bayport, all right," I said. "And we seem to be drifting right toward it."

Joe tilted his head. "There's just one problem."

"What?"

"I can't see the docks."

I looked again. Joe was right. The Bayport docks were nowhere in sight. "They must have been flooded by the hurricane," I said.

Joe sighed. "Go on and say it, Frank."

"Say what?"

"I told you so."

For the next hour or two, the waves carried us closer and closer to Bayport. Along the way, I told my brother that I didn't blame him for what happened. It was me, after all, who set off the camera flash and got us caught.

"So it's really all *your* fault, huh?" said Joe with a smirk.

"No, it's not *all* my fault," I said. "I *warned* you about Hurricane Herman. I *said* we should wait until the storm passed."

"In other words . . ."

"In other words . . . *I told you so*."

"I *knew* you'd say that, Frank."

I smacked him lightly on the back of his head.

"Hey! Don't mess with the hair!"

"Uh, I think the hurricane took care of that already." I glanced at the wild tangle of blond spikes sticking up from his scalp and started to laugh.

"Does it look that bad?" he asked.

"No, it looks *great*, Joe."

"It must be the new hair gel I'm using."

"Yeah, that must be it," I said, rolling my eyes. "But maybe you should stop worrying about your hair and start thinking about how we're going to get back on dry land."

We turned our attention to the shoreline—or what *used* to be the shoreline. The wooden docks were completely submerged in water. Some of the warehouses were flooded too, their arched roofs rising above the waves.

"Do you think the whole town is flooded?" Joe asked.

"No," I said. "Look at the storm wall over there. It's holding back the water."

I pointed toward the tall concrete wall that separated the docks from the main boardwalk.

"Hopefully the waves will carry us to the storm wall," I said as we floated into the bay.

The rain had completely stopped by now, but the waves were still pretty strong. Joe and I held on tightly to the Jet Ski as we swooshed past the flooded warehouses, heading straight for the storm wall. Unfortunately, every time we approached it, the waves pulled us right back into the bay.

"I'm starting to feel like a yo-yo," Joe grumbled.

"Maybe we should try jumping onto the roof of one of those warehouses," I suggested.

"Okay," Joe agreed. "Get ready. We're about to pass one now."

My brother and I hunched down. A big wave pushed us toward a flooded warehouse.

"Come on! Let's do it!" Joe shouted.

"We're not close enough!" I shouted back.

"We can do it!"

"No, we can't!"

Too late. We missed our chance.

The wave carried us along, faster and faster—hurling us straight toward a huge eighteen-wheel truck that was parked in the flooded lot.

"Look out! We're going to crash!" I yelled.

CRUNCH!

The wave slammed our Jet Ski into the side of the truck and tossed us like a pair of rag dolls onto the roof of the trailer. Then the wave retracted with a sudden *whoosh*, leaving us stranded on top of the eighteen-wheeler.

"Wow. That was kind of fun," said Joe, climbing to his feet. "Can we do it again?"

I sighed. "You might get your chance, Joe, if another wave comes along and slams us into the storm wall over there. That would be *tons* of fun."

"There you go again, Frank. Always looking on the bright side."

"Hey. *You* were the one who thought we'd get eaten by sharks."

"It could still happen. We're not out of the water yet."

I stood up and surveyed the area. The truck we were standing on was completely surrounded by water. In fact, the whole parking lot was flooded. The water level must have been about seven or eight feet.

"We could try to swim to the wall," Joe suggested.

I shook my head. "I don't like the looks of that current. It'll sweep us back into the bay."

"Well, I have another idea."

"What?"

"We could flag down that rescue boat over there."

I turned toward the docks and saw a small emergency rescue boat speeding between the warehouse roofs. Joe and I jumped up and down and started waving.

"Hey! Over here! Help!"

At first I thought they didn't see us. But then the boat turned and headed straight toward us. I could see two men on board, one of them holding a megaphone.

"We're coming to help you!" a deep voice boomed across the bay. "Do not panic! Stay right where you are!"

"Where does he think we're going?" Joe mumbled. "Candyland?"

I smacked my brother's arm. "Don't bite the hand that rescues you."

"Yeah, but give me a break. They must think we're stupid or something."

"Well, if the life preserver fits . . ."

Joe was about to protest when the rescue boat pulled up next to the eighteen-wheeler.

"Don't make any sudden moves! We're going to help you climb aboard!" the shorter guy bellowed into the megaphone.

The taller guy glared at his partner. "Put down the megaphone, Wilson. They can hear you."

"Oh, sorry."

I glanced at Joe and stifled a laugh. Our rescuers were incredibly young—and obviously inexperienced.

"Man, are we glad to see you," I told them.

The taller guy reached over and grabbed the edge of the truck while the smaller guy held out a brawny arm to help us aboard.

"Didn't you guys play football for Bayport High?" I asked, climbing into the boat.

"Yeah," said the smaller one. "Grady and I were Most Valuable Players two years in a row."

Joe's eyes lit up. "Of course! You're Billy Wilson! And you're Greg Grady! You guys are awesome!"

Wilson's round face turned red.

"Do you still play ball?" I asked.

Grady turned away, grabbing the wheel. "No. We couldn't get scholarships to college, so we decided to join the Emergency Rescue Team. At least it's physical."

"That's cool," said Joe.

Wilson sat back and smiled. "You guys should join up. You could be volunteers. That's how we got started."

Grady looked over his shoulder at us. "You're not afraid of a little danger, are you?"

I shot a quick look at Joe, who smiled back at me. "No, we're not afraid of danger," I said.

"Heck," said Joe. "We eat danger for breakfast."

Wilson and Grady laughed, then told us more about the Emergency Rescue Team. They said that the training was really tough and the pay was terrible, but there was nothing like saving lives to make you feel like a hero.

By the time we reached the main boardwalk, Joe and I were ready to sign up.

"Give us a call at the station sometime," said Wilson, shaking our hands. My brother and I hopped off the boat, happy to be back on dry land. Then Wilson and Grady said good-bye and sped away across the bay.

I looked at Joe. "So? Are you ready to see if the town is as damaged as your hair?"

"I thought you said my hair looked great."

"I lied."

Joe shot me a dirty look—and fussed with his spiky hair all the way back to town.

The town square was a total wreck.

I couldn't believe all the tree branches and debris littering the streets. Trash cans were overturned, road signs knocked askew. The gutters were completely overflowing with rainwater. Joe and I had to take running leaps to reach the parking lot by the bank.

"Good thing we parked our motorcycles on higher ground," said Joe, hopping on and revving his engine.

I put on my helmet. Then the two of us carefully made our way across the slippery streets of Bayport, swerving left and right to avoid some major puddles. A few minutes later we reached the outskirts of our neighborhood—and were surprised to see some of our neighbors walking down the street.

"Frank! Joe!"

The high-pitched voice made us stop in our tracks. Pulling off my helmet, I turned to see Belinda Conrad waving and strolling toward us. Her brother Brian was right behind her—sneering, as usual.

"Hi, losers," said Brian, as charming as ever.

"Ignore him," Belinda told us. "He's just grouchy because we've spent the last few hours in the high school gym. It was set up as an emergency evacuation center."

"Yeah, and it was crowded and smelly, too," Brian added. "I can't wait to take a shower." He turned and headed toward his house across the street.

Belinda shrugged and smiled, then glanced down at our clothes. "You guys are totally soaked! You weren't riding your motorcycles in this storm, were you? That's so dangerous."

I glanced at Joe. "No, we weren't riding motorcycles," I said. Of course, I didn't telling her we were riding *Jet Skis*.

Belinda was starting to ask another question when her brother came running out of the house, shaking his fists.

"Everything's gone!" he shouted.

Belinda looked at him and sighed. "What's gone, Brian?"

"The stereo! The TV! The computer!" he yelled.

Belinda looked confused. "What are you talking about?"

"Someone must have broken in after we evacuated," said Brian.

"You mean . . . ?"

"Yes! We've been robbed!"

3.
SOS

Robbed?

I just couldn't believe it.

What kind of creep would rob people during a natural disaster?

I took off my helmet, scratched my head, and scanned the area for clues.

Frank, in the meantime, tried to comfort Belinda—who was totally weirded out by the idea of intruders in her home. Her brother stood next to them, talking to the police on his cell phone.

"That's right, officer," Brian explained. "What? Three houses on Orchard Street robbed too? Yeah, we'll be here."

Minutes later a pair of squad cars pulled up to the house, sirens wailing and lights flashing. Four police officers got out and started questioning the neighbors. One of the officers, a lanky guy named Chen, pulled Frank and me aside to talk.

"I have a message from your father," he told us. "Bob and Peter Plotnik have been arrested. The Coast Guard recovered the toxic chemicals on the freighter and managed to wrangle a confession out of them."

"That's good," said Frank, "because I lost my camera when a wave knocked Joe and me off the Jet Ski."

"Butterfingers," I muttered under my breath.

"Helmet hair," he shot back, glancing up at my head.

Officer Chen looked at me and burst out laughing. Then he said good-bye and walked off, joining his fellow officers at the crime scene.

"It looks like they have this under control," Frank said. "Let's get out of here . . . before anyone else sees your hair."

On the way home, I kept thinking about the wild events of the day: the hurricane, the flooding, the burglaries.

What next? I wondered.

The answer was waiting for me inside our house: Aunt Trudy.

"You're tracking mud all over the place!" she screeched as soon as we walked through the door. "I just waxed these floors!"

Frank and I looked down and sighed.

"We're sorry, Aunt Trudy," I said.

"Well, you'll be even sorrier if you don't march outside right now and take off those filthy shoes!"

"We're going, we're going," I mumbled.

Frank and I trudged to the back porch, plopping down on a bench near the door. Our shoes were caked with mud, and our socks were soaking wet. As we tugged them off, the back door swung open and Dad joined us on the porch.

"Did you get my message?" he asked.

"Yeah, Dad," said Frank. "Officer Chen told us about the arrest."

"I'm sure all the guys down at the station will be glad to see the Plotniks finally behind bars. They've been trying to stop those toxic dumpers for a long time now."

Our father, Fenton Hardy, is a former policeman who came up with the idea for American Teens Against Crime. Even though he left the force a couple of years ago, he still stays in touch with his old buddies—and gets the inside story on all the wanted criminals in the area.

"You two look like drowned rats," he said,

noticing our wet clothes. "Come inside, dry off, and tell me what happened."

We went inside—and were immediately greeted by our squawking parrot, Playback, who sat on the back of Aunt Trudy's favorite armchair in the living room. Our aunt and Mom were huddled around the television, eyes glued to the screen.

"Hi, Mom," I said. "We're home."

She held up a finger. "Shhh. Johnny Thunder is about to give the local weather update."

"Who's Johnny Thunder?" I asked.

Mom responded with another "Shhh."

"He's the local reporter for the Weather Network," Frank whispered in my ear. "You'd know who he was if you had checked the weather before hopping on a Jet Ski."

"Don't rub it in."

We turned our attention to the TV. On the screen, a tall, overly tanned man with perfectly groomed hair and gleaming white teeth pointed to a map of the local area.

"There's been some flooding in the lower regions," he explained in a deep, booming voice. "The Bayport docks are almost completely underwater. But the town square hasn't suffered much damage, thanks to the storm wall."

He went on to report that the worst was over,

and water levels were already beginning to go down. Then he finished his broadcast with an exaggerated wink and a big, phony grin.

"This is Johnny Thunder," he gushed, "wishing you health, happiness, and happy weather."

What a ham.

Aunt Trudy sighed. "What a handsome man!"

"You've got to be kidding," I said, groaning. "He's a total cheese ball! Just look at his hair! It looks like it's molded out of plastic."

Aunt Trudy glared at me. "I wouldn't be talking about bad hair if I were you, Joe."

Mom started laughing. "Yeah, it looks like the hurricane did a real number on you. Where were you boys, anyway?"

I glanced at Frank and shrugged. "We were heading to the mall but got caught in the rain and had to pull over," I said, thinking fast.

Mom frowned. "I don't want you boys to ride your motorcycles during a hurricane alert."

"Yes, you should always tune in to Johnny Thunder before you leave the house," added Aunt Trudy. "He may have plastic-looking hair—but he really knows the weather."

Frank nudged my arm and gave me one of his *I told you so* looks.

Then Mom ordered us upstairs to shower and

change into some dry clothes. Frank and I turned and headed to the stairs, arguing over who would get to use the bathroom first.

"Race you for it!"

I knocked my brother aside and dashed up the steps two at a time. When I reached the bathroom, I was surprised to hear the shower running.

Who could be taking a shower? I wondered. *Everyone else is downstairs.*

Frank came up behind me, pointing at the bathroom door with a puzzled look on his face.

I shook my head and shrugged.

My brother put a finger to his lips, then gave the door a little push. It swung open with a soft squeak. We peeked inside. But all we could see was the shower curtain—pulled closed along the length of the bathtub.

"Hello?" said Frank.

No one answered.

Slowly we took a step inside.

"Hello?"

Nothing.

I reached for the shower curtain. Taking a deep breath, I pulled it open.

There was nobody there.

What's going on?

I glanced down. The bathtub was filled almost

to the brim with water. Floating on top was a shoebox-size package tied to a small inflatable life preserver.

The package was marked "SOS."

I looked at Frank. "Another mission?"

"Sure looks like it." My brother leaned down. Turning off the shower and unplugging the drain, he pulled the package out of the water and handed it to me.

"Here. Take this," he said. "I'm taking a shower."

Then, with a little shove, he pushed me out of the bathroom and locked the door.

Twenty minutes later we were clean, dry, and ready to take on our next assignment. Frank fired up the computer while I opened the package with a pocketknife.

"What does SOS stand for, anyway?" I asked.

My brother leaned back in his chair. "It doesn't stand for any specific words. It comes from Morse code: dot-dot-dot, dash-dash-dash, dot-dot-dot. The letters SOS are easy to transmit. That's why they were selected by the International Radio-telegraphic Convention at Berlin in 1906."

"Gee, thanks, Mr. Know-It-All. Any other useless knowledge you'd like to share?"

"I'm glad you asked, Joe." Frank smiled and continued the lecture. "The U.S. Coast Guard no longer monitors Morse code messages. The distress code they use is Mayday, taken from the French phrase *m'aider*, meaning 'help me.'"

I stared at my brother, shaking my head. "You're such a nerd, Frank."

"Just open the package, Joe."

I reached inside the box and pulled out a pair of ultraslim inflatable life vests, a mini "weather tracker" device with satellite hookup, and a hand-cranked emergency radio. At the bottom of the box was a CD labeled "SOS," which I handed to Frank.

He popped it into his computer, then pressed a button. I pulled up a chair and waited for the show to begin.

KER-BOOM!

A roar of thunder erupted from the speakers. Then a bolt of lightning lit up the screen. Dark stormy images of clouds, rain, and wind flashed before our eyes—a steady flow of news clips of recent storms and disasters.

"Hurricanes," a voice announced grimly. *"Every year they wreak havoc in coastal communities, cutting a dangerous path of destruction wherever they go. The winds of a Category One hurricane range from seventy-*

four to ninety-five miles per hour and can cause minor damage and flooding. The most severe hurricanes, Category Five, have winds greater than 155 miles per hour. They can destroy small buildings and much worse. Anyone living within five to ten miles of the shoreline should evacuate their homes immediately."

We were shown pictures of emergency evacuation centers crowded with families, rescue workers, and rows of sleeping cots. Then the images faded, and a map of the United States filled the screen.

"Hurricanes begin as storm depressions, usually in tropical regions," the voice continued. "The most commonly affected areas include the Gulf Coast and the Southern states along the Atlantic."

The Doppler radar showed the swirling movements of massive clouds sweeping over the coasts.

"Sometimes, due to various weather conditions, hurricanes can hit the Northeast as well. This summer, according to meteorologists, a series of storms could cause large-scale damage from Virginia to Maine. So far, the hurricanes have not been severe. But local communities aren't taking any chances. Citizens are routinely evacuated when a storm threatens to strike."

The map was replaced with a video of families shielding their heads from the rain as they entered a large building.

"Hey! That's Bayport High School," I said.

The voice continued. *"Mother Nature isn't the only problem. This past week, area homes have been burglarized after the owners evacuated. There have been four break-ins in Seacrest and five in Eastwood. Just today there were three more burglaries in Bayport."*

I glanced at Frank. He was shaking his head.

"The ATAC team believes this is the worst kind of crime," the voice went on. *"The burglars are taking advantage of a terrible situation—and they have to be stopped. Your mission, Joe and Frank, is to get to the bottom of all this. These criminals must be caught as soon as possible. Otherwise, the public may refuse to evacuate their homes for fear of being robbed. Their lives could be in danger."*

The screen went black.

"This CD will be erased in exactly five seconds. Good luck, boys."

A few moments later the disk reformatted itself and music blared from the computer's speakers.

It was the song "Rock You Like a Hurricane."

Frank spun around in his chair. "Well, it looks like we stumbled right into our next mission without even knowing it."

"Yeah, just our luck." I reached for the emergency radio that was packed inside the box and started turning the hand crank. After a few twists, the radio buzzed to life. "Check it out. This little baby can tune in to TV stations."

I played with the knobs for a while, trying to find a better channel. First there was nothing but static. Then a deep voice began to deliver the local weather report.

"That's Johnny Thunder," said Frank. "Turn it up."

I adjusted the volume and listened.

"This is Johnny Thunder with a special emergency broadcast. You may be relieved to learn that Hurricane Herman has changed direction and is headed out to sea. But the danger is not over yet. I is repeat: The danger is not over yet."

I glanced nervously at Frank.

Johnny Thunder continued. "A more severe storm is gathering strength off the Northeast coast. Her name is Hurricane Ivy. And she's heading right for us."

4.
Weather or Not

"Emergency! Emergency!"

Playback squawked and swooped and circled over my bed, his wings fluttering in the morning light.

I glanced at my clock radio and groaned.

"Six thirty? Go back to sleep, Playback."

The parrot landed on the headboard above me. "Emergency!" he screeched again—loudly.

I rubbed my eyes and gazed out the window. The sky was clear and blue, sunlight streaming through the trees. "It sure doesn't look like an emergency," I muttered, staring up at the bird. "Have you been watching Johnny Thunder with Aunt Trudy again?"

"Yes, he has."

Aunt Trudy stuck her head through the door and winked.

"I sent Playback in here to wake you up," she said. "We have a lot of work to do today."

I yawned. "Yeah? Like what?"

"Johnny Thunder said Hurricane Ivy might become a Category Three or Four—so I want you boys to storm-proof this house."

I swung my legs over the side of the bed. "What do you want us to do?"

"Not much. Just tape some Xs over the windows, and nail down the loose shutters, and move the lawn furniture into the garage."

"Oh. Is that all?" I said, sighing.

"No, that's not all. I'll give you further instructions over breakfast." Aunt Trudy clicked her fingers, and Playback flew across the room, landing on her shoulder. "Hurry up and get dressed, Frank. I'll go wake up your brother. We need to be prepared in case of an emergency."

Playback flapped his wings. "Emergency! Emergency!" he kept squawking as they left the room.

"Aunt Trudy! Wait!" I called after her.

She stopped and turned around. "Yes, Frank?"

"Can I watch you wake up Joe?"

Aunt Trudy gave me a sly smile. Then, laughing

quietly, we carried Playback down the hall to Joe's bedroom.

Somebody was in for a rude awakening.

"Emergency!"

After his little wake-up call, Joe was a total grouch all morning long. He grumbled and complained through every task Aunt Trudy gave us.

"I don't know why we have to do this," he said, standing in the grass below the ladder. "There's not a cloud in the sky."

I looked up. Joe was right. The noonday sun was blazing overhead. The heat had even managed to dry up the rain from yesterday's storm.

"Just hold the ladder for me," I said, bracing myself on the top step. "This is the last shutter."

My brother glared at me. "Why should I?"

"Um, because I might *fall*."

"It would serve you right," he said, "for waking me up like that today."

"Hey, Playback woke me up the same way. It's not my fault you woke up screaming like a little girl."

"I did *not* scream like a little girl."

"Aunt Trudy!" I shouted down through the kitchen window.

Aunt Trudy peeked out. "Yes?"

"Didn't Joe scream like a little girl this morning?"

She burst out laughing. "Oh, my, yes! Just like a little girl!"

Playback hopped onto her shoulder. "Little girl! Little girl!" he squawked.

Aunt Trudy and I howled—while Joe turned red.

"Go on and laugh," he growled. "I'll get you back, and your little bird, too. When you least expect it." He reached out and steadied the ladder. "Nail in that shutter, Frank. And make it fast."

I wasn't going to argue—not while I was standing on the top rung and he was holding the ladder. Reaching up, I pounded in a few more nails until the shutter was secure. Then I climbed down and helped Joe carry the ladder back to the garage.

"So how are we going to catch these burglars, Frank?"

I shrugged. "I don't know. We don't have any clues to go on."

"No suspects, either," Joe added.

"Maybe we should talk to Belinda and Brian. The burglars might have left a clue in their house."

"Like fingerprints?"

"Yeah, but they probably used gloves. Otherwise the police would have a lead on them already."

Joe scratched his head. "Maybe one of the neighbors saw something."

"They were evacuated, remember?"

Joe sighed. "Okay, so no witnesses, no suspects, and no clues—yet. That means we have to catch the burglars in the act."

I thought about it. "The chances of that are pretty slim, Joe. If there's another evacuation, every house in town will be a target. We can try to keep an eye on things, but we can't be everywhere at once."

"I know one thing," said Joe.

"What?"

"I'm starving."

As if on cue, Aunt Trudy hollered at us from the kitchen window. "Come and get it, boys!"

Joe and I headed for the back door, glancing up again at the bright blue sky.

"I still find it hard to believe there's a hurricane coming," said Joe.

"We can check the weather report again."

I opened the door and walked to the kitchen counter. Aunt Trudy had laid out a whole smorgasbord of cold cuts, cheese, fruit, and macaroni salad.

"We're eating in front of the TV," she told us, putting food on her plate. "The Weather Network is covering Hurricane Ivy, and I don't want to miss it."

"You don't want to miss Johnny Thunder," I said. "Admit it, Aunt Trudy."

She pursed her lips. "Well, he *is* awfully handsome." Then she carried her plate out of the room.

Joe shook his head. "I never even heard of this Johnny Thunder guy until yesterday. What kind of name is that, anyway? I bet he made it up."

"You think?"

We loaded up our plates and headed out to the living room. Mom, Dad, and Aunt Trudy sat on the sofa in front of folding TV trays, their eyes glued to the set. Playback was perched on top of the television, preening and posing. He seemed to think everyone was looking at *him*, not Johnny Thunder.

Joe and I sat down in a pair of armchairs and balanced our plates on our laps. I expected Aunt Trudy to snap at us for spilling crumbs—but she was totally mesmerized by the "awfully handsome" weatherman on the screen.

Johnny Thunder stood in front of the docks, wearing a yellow rain slicker and holding a large microphone. "According to our meteorologists, Hurricane Ivy is gathering strength along the northeast coast," he said. "We strongly urge you to evacuate your homes now, before the storm reaches Bayport."

Mom looked skeptical. "But it's so beautiful outside," she said, pointing to the window. "Maybe they've made a mistake."

Aunt Trudy reacted with a loud huff. "Johnny Thunder is *never* wrong."

Joe and I stood up and walked to the window. "He might be wrong this time, Aunt Trudy," I said, scanning the sky. "If Hurricane Ivy is only twenty miles away, there should be some clouds overhead."

"You're not a meteorologist, Frank," she replied. "If Johnny Thunder says we should evacuate, we should listen to him."

Dad stood up and joined us at the window. "I don't think that will be necessary, Trudy," he said. "We should be okay here. The boys storm-proofed the house, and we're on higher ground than the rest of the town."

A commercial for breakfast cereal came on the TV. Aunt Trudy picked up the remote and started flipping through the channels.

I whispered to Joe, "If people evacuate their homes, there could be more burglaries."

Joe was about to respond when Aunt Trudy interrupted.

"This is strange," she said.

We turned around. "What is?"

"None of the other channels are covering Hurricane Ivy. Their weathermen are still talking about Hurricane Herman. There's no mention of Ivy at all."

We sat down and watched a few of the broadcasts.

Aunt Trudy was right.

Nobody was predicting another hurricane—except the Weather Network.

Joe and I were stumped.

Something was going on—something highly suspicious—and we were determined to get to the bottom of it. That's why we snuck out the back door after we took our empty plates to the kitchen.

"Just look at that sky," said Joe, shielding his eyes from the bright sun. "This has to be one of the nicest days of the summer."

I had to agree.

But many of our neighbors were putting their trust in Johnny Thunder's weather report. The streets were filled with families packing up their cars to head to the emergency evacuation center.

"The high school is in the other direction, boys," our neighbor, Mr. Benton, pointed out.

"You don't want to get caught in the storm."

We thanked him for his concern but kept walking down the street. A couple of blocks later, we ran into our friend Chet Morton. He was heading toward us with his parents and his sister, Iola, who was home from performing arts school for the summer.

"Yo! Frank! Joe!" he shouted and waved. "Are you ready for another hurricane?"

We strolled over and said hi to his family.

Mrs. Morton stuffed a bottle of water into her husband's backpack. "Aren't you boys going to the evacuation center?" she asked.

"Soon," I said. "We still have a few hours."

"That's what I told her," said Chet. "We have plenty of time."

"You just want to stay home and play with your new Zbox," said Iola.

Joe's jaw dropped. "You got the new Zbox?"

Chet grinned. "Yup. I've been saving up for it all summer."

"And? Does it rock?"

"Totally. Want to check it out?"

Chet's mother sighed. "Not now, Chet."

"*Please?* It'll only take a minute, Mom," said Chet, pleading. "Five minutes. I'll catch up with you later."

She looked at Chet's father, who glanced up at the sky and shrugged. "Okay. Five minutes. That's all."

Chet let out a whoop and led us back to his house at the end of the block. Every step of the way, he babbled on about his Zbox and all the new games he'd bought for it. Joe was hanging on his every word.

Finally we reached the house. Chet ran up the stairs, crossed the porch, and froze.

"That's weird," he said with a confused look. "The door is open."

The three of us stood there in silence, staring at the wide-open door. I looked at Joe and Chet. Then, carefully, quietly, we tiptoed into the house.

The living room was empty. No intruders in sight.

No TV set, either.

"No way," Chet muttered slowly. "My Zbox! It's *gone! No!*"

His voice echoed through the house. For a few seconds we just stood there in shock. Nobody moved or spoke.

Then we heard footsteps in the kitchen.

And voices.

Were the burglars still around?

5.

Thunder Blunder

The next sound we heard was the back door open-
ing and slamming.

They're getting away!

I charged out of the room. Frank and Chet
scrambled after me as I dashed down the hall,
through the kitchen, and straight for the door.
Flinging it open, I jumped out and looked around.

Where did they go?

"Quick! Split up!" yelled Frank.

Chet took off toward the front of the house,
Frank ran around the back, and I sprinted toward
the bushes that lined the neighbor's yard. For a
second I thought I saw someone—but it was just a
shrub blowing in the wind.

They must be around here somewhere.

I circled the block a few times but finally gave up and headed back to Chet's house.

"Any luck?" asked Frank, jogging toward me.

"No. You?"

"No."

I kicked a pebble across the street. "Man! I can't believe we let them get away. They were right there in the house with us! We could hear them talking!"

"Don't beat yourself up about it, Joe," said Frank, slapping my arm. "At least now we know there's more than one burglar."

"So?" I said. "There's more than one Hardy."

The rest of the day was uneventful. No burglaries. No arrests. No clues.

No Hurricane Ivy, either.

After Chet called the cops to report the burglary, Frank and I walked home, wolfed down our dinner, and went to bed early. We were tired and achy from doing Aunt Trudy's chores. And after all that work she made us do, it never even rained.

"Better safe than sorry," she told us.

The following week, the weather was beautiful.

Then, one morning, I was woken by the sound of rain against my bedroom window.

It must be Hurricane Ivy, I thought. *Finally.*

I headed downstairs for breakfast and, once again, my family was gathered around the TV set. "Are you still watching Johnny Thunder?" I asked.

Dad looked up. "No. Johnny Thunder messed up last week—big-time. It turns out there never *was* a Hurricane Ivy."

"What?" I said.

Frank gave me a look. "Johnny told everyone to evacuate," he said. "And there was no hurricane."

"That's weird," I said.

"Yes, isn't it?" Frank agreed.

Aunt Trudy shook her head. "Someone must have slipped Johnny Thunder the wrong information. He should have listened to Playback instead."

"What do you mean?" I asked, glancing at the parrot.

"Playback always ruffles his feathers when a storm is coming," she explained. "He was completely calm yesterday. But look at him now."

Playback fluttered and fluffed up his feathers. A gust of wind and rain shook the windows.

I pointed outside and asked, "So, Hurricane Ivy is showing up a week late?"

Mom handed me a glass of juice. "No, it's not Ivy. There is no Ivy," she said. "But Hurricane

Irene is hitting the Southern states today, and we're feeling the side effects."

I walked to the front door and stared outside. Frank came up behind me. "I think we need to pay a visit to Johnny Thunder," he whispered.

I reached for my jacket on the coatrack. "I'm with you, bro."

As we walked toward the garage, Mom came running out onto the front porch. "Wait!" she shouted. "You boys are *not* riding your motorcycles in this rain!"

"But Mom," I groaned. "We have to, um, take care of something."

She shook her head. "The roads are too slippery."

Aunt Trudy stepped onto the porch. "They can take my Volkswagen," she offered. "It floats, you know."

"You're kidding," I said.

"No, I'm not," she said. "The old Volkswagen Beetles float in water. And the new tires get good traction in the rain."

Mom gave in. "Okay. But drive carefully. Some of the roads might be flooded."

We assured her we'd be careful. Aunt Trudy

tossed the keys to Frank, and we climbed inside the green Volkswagen. My brother handed me his backpack as he buckled himself into the driver's seat.

"What's in here?" I asked, peeking inside.

"My thirty-five millimeter camera, a tape recorder, and a notepad and pen."

I gave him a funny look. "What for?"

Frank explained as he drove. "Johnny Thunder is a big star—with a big ego. We can tell him we're huge fans of his, and we want to interview him for the first fall issue of the school newspaper. We'll say we're doing a story on Bayport High's most successful graduates. He'll eat it up."

"You're probably right," I said. "I have the feeling Johnny Thunder spends a lot of time in front of the mirror, fussing with his hair."

"See? You two have a lot in common," said Frank. "This should be a piece of cake."

It didn't take long for us to find the Weather Network offices in Eastwood—thanks to the giant satellite tower looming over the town. But getting to see Johnny Thunder was a whole other story.

"Johnny Thunder is not granting any interviews at this time," we were told by a thin, black-haired receptionist with cat's-eye glasses. "If you have questions about the Hurricane Ivy incident, the station manager sent out a press release last week."

Frank leaned over the reception desk. "I'm sorry, miss, but we're not here to ask about that. We're from the *Bayport High School News*. We're doing a feature article on Bayport's biggest success stories."

He flashed a big smile and—believe it or not—the receptionist started to blush.

I don't know how he does it. I'm *the good-looking one.*

I stepped up next to Frank. "Johnny Thunder is a hero for young people in the community." I flashed her my best smile, but she wouldn't take her eyes off Frank.

I give up.

"Me? Johnny Thunder? A hero?"

Frank and I spun around—and there he was. Johnny Thunder. Trusted weatherman. Beloved TV personality.

And criminal mastermind?

He reached out his hand. "It's always a pleasure to meet my young fans," he said in a ridiculously deep voice. "I believe that children are the future—and it's important to provide them with good role models."

Give me a break.

We shook his hand, and before we knew it, the guy was ushering Frank and me into his gigantic corner office. "Make yourselves comfortable," he said, offering us a seat on a big leather sofa.

Frank pulled out his tape recorder and notepad. "First, I'd like to ask you about your background."

Johnny smiled and leaned against his desk, stroking his lantern-shaped jaw. "Growing up in Bayport, I was just a little boy with big dreams. My mind was always bursting with questions. Every day I would lie on the docks and look up at the sky, filled with awe and wonder. I'd watch the clouds and ask myself, 'What does it all mean?'"

It means you're a total windbag, I thought, settling in for what promised to be the world's longest interview.

"That was just the beginning of my lifelong obsession with the weather," he went on. "When I was eight, I started making charts of the cloud movements over Bayport, and then I . . ."

His voice droned on and on. I seriously thought I was going to fall asleep, but then—forty minutes later—Johnny started talking about his job at the Weather Network.

Finally.

"My goal was to reinvent the weather report,"

he explained. "I wanted drama and excitement, action and adventure. I was prepared to do *anything* to grab the viewer's attention . . . and get bigger ratings."

I sat there, stunned.

Did Johnny just admit that he would "do anything" to boost his ratings?

Yes, he did.

Frank shot me a sideways glance. I knew immediately what he was thinking.

Johnny Thunder is definitely a prime suspect.

Johnny talked on and on about his "dazzling" career and "well-deserved" fame. Meanwhile, Frank and I fidgeted in our seats, dying to ask him some questions that could prove—or disprove—his connection to the burglaries.

Finally Frank managed to interrupt. "Excuse me, Mr. Thunder? Where do you get your weather information?"

"What do you mean?" he asked.

"I mean, how do you find out about things like hurricanes?" asked Frank. "Who told you that there was a hurricane named Ivy and that it was heading our way?"

Johnny Thunder buried his face in his hands. "I can't believe you're asking me this," he said,

SUSPECT PROFILE

Name: John Gooch, aka "Johnny Thunder"

Hometown: Bayport

Physical description: 35 years old, 6'2", 185 lbs., blond, perfectly styled hair, blue eyes, wears tailored suits in pastel colors to match his eyes.

Occupation: Weatherman

Background: Grew up in Bayport's richest neighborhood; spoiled by his doting mother; a teacher's pet in school; president of the Drama Club, Glee Club, and Future Millionaires of America; excellent student—but hated and teased by his peers.

Suspicious behavior: Reported false news about a hurricane that didn't exist.

Suspected of: Aiding burglars by urging people to evacuate their homes.

Possible motives: Money, ratings, revenge against former classmates.

groaning. "Every reporter in town wants to interview me about the mistake we made last week. I thought I could trust a pair of nice boys like you."

Frank leaned forward. "Don't worry, Mr.

Thunder. We won't use it in our article. I promise. I'm just curious how it how happened."

Johnny looked up and sighed. "I only report what I'm told by the Weather Network's control center."

"Who's in charge of the control center?" I asked.

Johnny rolled his eyes. "A funny little man named Irwin Link. He's a computer geek who works in the tower over there."

He pointed through his office window at the giant tower on the hill.

"Irwin gathers weather data from various satellites around the world," Johnny explained. "If anyone is to blame for the Hurricane Ivy slipup, it's Irwin Link."

I noticed Frank writing something in his notepad.

Johnny stared out the window, shaking his head. "That little weasel. It's all his fault. But nobody is blaming *him*. They're blaming Johnny Thunder. Did you read this morning's headline in the *Bayport Post*? It called Hurricane Ivy a 'Thunder Blunder.'"

Johnny rubbed his eyes, then lowered them. I have to admit: I was starting to feel sorry for the guy.

Then I looked at Frank. I could tell he felt the same way.

"Hand me your backpack, Frank," I said.

"What for?"

"I need the camera," I said. "I want to get some good pictures of Mr. Thunder for our article."

Johnny raised his head and spun around. His whole face lit up like a Christmas tree.

"Pictures! Of course," he said, beaming. "How would you like me to pose?"

6.
The Missing Link

Johnny Thunder's "photo shoot" took even longer than his "interview." Afterward, Joe and I headed back to the lobby of the TV station. Strolling up to the main desk, we stopped and talked to the receptionist with the cat's-eye glasses.

"Hello again," said Joe, leaning over the desk. "Could you do us a little favor? Could you tell us where to find Irwin Link?" He tilted his head and winked at her.

Oh, brother, I thought.

I hated it when Joe tried to be a ladies' man.

The receptionist wasn't impressed. "Do you have an appointment with Mr. Link?" she asked with a frown.

I jumped into the conversation. "No, we don't

have an appointment, miss. But we really need to talk to him. It's for our school paper." Then I lowered my voice and added, "Between you and me, I could use the extra credit."

The receptionist blushed and smiled at me. "Oh, all right. Irwin Link works in the weather tower on the hill behind us. Just take a right out of the parking lot, then circle around to the back."

We thanked her and headed outside.

Joe smacked my arm. "Why did you butt in back there? I could have gotten the info out of her."

"Yeah, right," I said. "All the ladies love those smooth moves you've got."

"Well, I *am* the popular one, Frank."

"Sure you are, Joe."

The rain was coming down harder now. We made a quick dash to Aunt Trudy's Volkswagen but still got totally soaked. Once we were inside the car, we discussed our little "interview" with Johnny Thunder.

"I think he's innocent," said Joe. "Did you see his face when you mentioned the Hurricane Ivy screwup? He was seriously upset."

"I agree. Johnny is too concerned about his image to blow it by lying about the weather."

I steered the car out of the parking lot and circled around the main building. A moment later I spotted the weather tower, jutting up from the side of a steep hill. Its narrow concrete base rose up about three or four stories tall and was topped with a huge steel-grid spire.

"Oooh, scary," said Joe, gazing upward. "Looks like Frankenstein's laboratory."

"Yeah, especially in this rainstorm."

I pulled up in front of the tower, parking the Volkswagen next to an old beat-up Ford sedan. A small sign read: RESERVED FOR IRWIN LINK.

Joe pointed at the Ford's rusty fender. "It looks like Irwin doesn't get paid very well."

"At least he has his own parking space."

"Yeah, right near the Dumpsters."

We climbed out of the car and ran through the rain to the entrance. Joe grabbed the handle of a large steel door and pulled—but it was locked. So I pressed a button on a small intercom box.

"Hello? Who's there?" said a crackly voice.

"Mr. Link?" I shouted into the box.

"Yes?"

"This is Frank and Joe Hardy. We're students from Bayport High School, and we're writing a paper on meteorology. Could you help us out?"

"I'm very busy," the voice replied. Then there

was a short pause. "Oh, what the heck. I suppose I can talk for a few minutes."

Seconds later, a loud buzzing sound opened the steel door. Joe and I stepped inside, the door slamming shut behind us. After our eyes adjusted to the darkness, we found ourselves standing at the bottom of a concrete stairwell.

"Up here!" a voice shouted over our heads.

We looked up. A skinny little man with thick glasses and thinning hair leaned over the railing forty feet above us. He gestured with his hand, then disappeared.

"Dr. Frankenstein, I presume?" Joe muttered under his breath.

"Shhh." I smacked my brother's arm and started climbing the stairs.

Irwin was waiting for us at the top landing. Shaking our hands awkwardly, he led us into a room that was jam-packed with all sorts of electronic equipment—computers, monitors, radar screens, fax machines, and a whole bunch of stuff I couldn't identify.

"What do you boys want to know?" he asked, sitting down in a rolling office chair.

I looked around for a place to sit, but there wasn't any. So I took a deep breath and asked what I *thought* was a very simple question. "How do you collect data for your weather forecasts?"

Irwin clapped his hands together. "Here at the Weather Network, we use a wide variety of sources, including satellites, radars, local and national weather centers, and my own calculations."

He went on and on, describing his sources and methods in great detail, pointing to the various gadgets and gizmos around the room. The more he talked, the more excited he got. His glasses started sliding down his nose, and his wispy hair stood up on end. He looked just like a mad scientist in a scary movie.

Dr. Frankenstein.

After fifteen minutes of listening to Irwin's long, drawn-out lecture, I just had to interrupt.

"What about Johnny Thunder, Mr. Link?" I asked. "Doesn't he help you with the weather forecasts?"

Irwin scowled and spun around in his chair. "Johnny Thunder," he scoffed. "Johnny Thunder doesn't know *anything* about the weather. He's just a puppet with pretty hair who reads from cue cards."

"Really?" I said. "I thought he was a highly respected weatherman."

"A well-trained poodle is more like it," Irwin sneered. "The network wanted a handsome face to report the weather, not a *real* meteorologist—like me. Let's face it. No one wants to look at *me*. Why do you think I'm stuck in this little tower behind the main building? Because I'm smart enough to *predict* the weather but not good-looking enough to *report* it."

Irwin slammed his fist on the desk. I glanced at Joe and thought, *We have our second suspect.*

Irwin stopped speaking. So I decided to get right to the point.

"What about Hurricane Ivy?" I asked. "How could you broadcast warnings about a hurricane that didn't even exist?"

Irwin raised his head and looked at me. "I'm still trying to figure out what went wrong," he said softly. "Someone must have hacked into the Weather Network's mainframe to feed me false information."

"Who could have done that?" I asked.

Irwin shrugged his bony shoulders. "I don't know. My computer system is directly linked to the local police, fire department, rescue units, Coast Guard, and other government agencies. We share a lot of information, in case of an emergency."

Joe cleared his throat. "So who sent you the data about Hurricane Ivy?"

Irwin sighed. "I'm not sure. It looked like a typical warning from the National Weather Service. But then, when I realized it was a hoax, I

SUSPECT PROFILE

Name: Irwin Link

Hometown: Elizabeth, NJ

Physical description: 42 years old, 5'6", 125 lbs., brown, wispy hair, thick glasses, wears ill-fitting clothes, drives a rusty beat-up Ford.

Occupation: Meteorologist

Background: Attended Eastwood High School, graduated with top honors, worked his way through college and received his master's degree in meteorology, then found that no television news show would put him in front of the cameras.

Suspicious behavior: Displayed extreme anger and jealousy over Johnny Thunder's fame and popularity.

Suspected of: Purposely lying about Hurricane Ivy, and possibly scheming with local criminals.

Possible motives: Revenge against Johnny Thunder and the Weather Network, extra money to supplement his low pay.

tried to trace it back to the source."

"And?"

"It couldn't be traced."

I was starting to ask another question when one of the monitors started flashing and beeping. Irwin spun around in his chair, leaning forward and studying the screen.

"What is it?" I asked.

"It's Hurricane Irene," he said, biting his lip. "She's heading north along the coast, moving at an incredible speed. This could be a real disaster. I'm talking Category Four."

I looked at Joe. "Maybe we should head home."

We thanked Irwin for his time and started to leave. "Be careful, boys!" he shouted after us. "Conditions are pretty bad out there!"

Joe and I scrambled down the concrete stairwell, flung open the door, and ran outside.

Whoosh!

The rain hit us like a tidal wave, the wind almost knocking us off our feet. Joe and I had to lower our heads as we charged toward the Volkswagen. Joe jumped in first on the driver's side. Then he reached over to open the passenger door.

"Hurry, Frank! Get in!"

Fighting the wind, I climbed inside and slammed the door. "Now *this* looks like a hurricane!" I said, gasping.

"Yeah, we'd better get moving," said Joe. "Give me the keys."

"You're driving? In this storm?"

He shrugged. "If we wait any longer, the roads might be flooded."

Joe had a point. I tossed him the keys, and he revved up the engine. Then, flipping on the windshield wipers, he pulled out of the lot and headed for the highway back to Bayport.

"Turn on the headlights," I said, squinting at the dark, wet road.

Joe flicked on the lights, but it didn't make much difference. The sky was almost black with clouds, and raindrops riddled the car like bullets. The windshield wipers were practically useless.

"Slow down," I warned Joe.

"Don't worry. I have it under control."

I turned my head and noticed a little lake surrounded by cottages. The water was wild and choppy—and rising fast. At one end of the lake, a small man-made damn was totally overflowing and gushing into a small river.

This doesn't look good.

My eyes followed the trail of the river. It ran parallel with the road for about a hundred feet, then swooped toward a small bridge directly in front of us. Water smashed against the guardrails— and splashed onto the road.

"Joe! Stop the car!" I yelled.

Joe slammed down hard on the brakes.

But it was too late.

The Volkswagen's wheels spun in the water as we skimmed across the flooded bridge. Then the back end of the car swung around and flung us toward the guardrail.

"Hold on!" I shouted.

The Volkswagen smashed through the rail. *CRRRRUNCH!*

Then we hurtled over the side of the bridge.

7.

In Case of Emergency

SPLASH!

The car hit the water like a sumo wrestler doing a belly flop into a baby pool. Giant waves shot up around us, streaking the windows on all four sides of the Volkswagen. The car plunged downward, deeper and deeper.

We're sinking, I thought.

Frank muttered something about life vests and started digging into his backpack.

Me? I braced myself for a rocky landing on the bottom of the river.

Here we go.

But instead of sinking deeper, the Volkswagen jerked and jolted upward.

Whoosh!

We shot out of the water like a rocket, then bobbed up and down on the surface.

"Frank! We're floating!" I shouted.

My brother glanced up from his backpack. "Wow. Aunt Trudy was right," he mumbled.

The current of the river carried us along, rocking the Volkswagen back and forth in the churning waves. Thankfully, the windshield wipers were still working, and so was the motor. But when I pressed the gas, the wheels just spun in the water.

"Now what?" I asked. "How are we going to get out of this river?"

"Maybe we'll drift toward the edge," said Frank.

In the meantime, I had no choice but to just sit and wait. Hunched over the steering wheel, I watched carefully as we drifted downstream.

"We've been floating for a long time," I said, starting to get worried.

Just then, I felt a little bump beneath the car. We pivoted in the water, and the car spun slowly toward the edge of the river. Then I felt another bump.

"We're making contact," said Frank. "Hit the gas."

I pushed down on the accelerator. The Volkswagen's wheels spun a few times, then grabbed hold in the rocky riverbed.

Vroooom!

The car bounced and slowly crawled out of the shallow water. Soon we were up on the riverbank, driving across a wet field of grass. .

"Which way?" I asked.

Frank pointed to the right. "I think the road is back that way."

After some slipping and sliding in the mud, I was able to reach the main road back to Bayport. The rain was still coming down hard, making it hard to see, but I was relieved to be back on concrete again.

"Bayport, three miles," I said, reading a road sign.

Frank was about to say something when his cell phone rang. He pulled it out of his Windbreaker and answered the call. "Hello? Yes . . . What? Where? Don't worry. Joe and I are on the way!" Then he hung up.

"Who was that?" I asked.

"Mom and Aunt Trudy," he answered grimly. "They're trapped on the roof of Hiller's Hardware Store."

"Whoa. What happened?"

"The storm wall broke. The town square is totally flooded."

When we reached Bayport, Frank told me to drive to our friend Chet's house. Why? Because he wanted to borrow Chet's motorboat to rescue Mom and Aunt Trudy.

"No problem," said Chet. "As long as I can come along to help."

We followed him out to his garage and hooked up the small motorboat trailer to the back of the Volkswagen. Then we headed for the town square.

"Why didn't your family evacuate your home?" I asked our friend on the way. "Hurricane Irene looks like the real deal. Category three or four."

"My family's worried about getting burglarized again," he told us. "According to the news, over twenty homes were robbed after people evacuated for that fake Hurricane Ivy."

I drove the car to the edge of the town square and then quickly pulled to a stop—because the rest of the road was completely underwater. Frank and I helped Chet unlatch the boat from the trailer and carry it to the square. Once we were knee-deep in water, we hopped inside and Chet revved up the outboard motor.

"Where are they?" asked Chet.

Frank pointed him in the direction of Hiller's Hardware Store on the far end of the square.

"Look! There they are!" I shouted, pointing up at the figures standing on the roof of the store.

Chet gunned the engine. The boat picked up speed as we glided past flooded mailboxes, parking meters, and stranded cars. Soon we were close enough to make out the figures.

"Hold on! We're on our way!" I yelled upward.

Mom and Aunt Trudy waved back at us. Standing right behind them was Mr. Hiller, owner of the hardware store.

Chet pulled the motorboat alongside the building and stopped. I gazed up at the roof. The eaves were about ten feet over our heads, and I wondered how we were going to get everybody down.

Mr. Hiller peered over the side. "Thanks for coming!" he shouted. "Now all you have to do is help us climb down."

Frank pointed to the drainpipe. "Maybe you can shimmy down that."

"Or we could use this," said Mr. Hiller, dangling an emergency rope ladder from the roof. "I grabbed it from the store when the water started coming in."

Chet and Frank grabbed the end of the rope ladder and pulled it taut. Then we saw a pair of women's legs reach out from the eaves.

"Where's the rung? I can't find the rung!"

It was Aunt Trudy. I recognized her voice—and her bright yellow rain boots kicking wildly in the air. Finally one of her feet hooked onto a rung of the ladder. Then her rear end appeared over the side of the roof, followed by the rest of her body. Mr. Hiller held onto her until she had a good grip on the ladder. Slowly she began climbing down.

"I got you, Aunt Trudy," I said, reaching up. I wrapped my arms around her waist and helped her down.

"Oh, that tickles, Joe."

She giggled and stepped off the ladder, then took a seat at the back of the boat. I looked up again to see my mother starting to climb down. About halfway she stopped and closed her eyes.

"I hate heights," she grumbled.

"Don't worry, Mom. I got you." I stretched up my arms and helped her the rest of the way.

Mr. Hiller was next. He was a pretty athletic guy, so he didn't have much trouble. Once everyone was sitting in the boat, Mom told us what had happened. "Aunt Trudy and I came here to pick up some emergency supplies, and then the storm wall broke. The square was flooded in ten minutes flat, and then the water started gushing into the store."

"Did you call 911?" asked Frank.

She shook her head. "The water level was pretty low, so we weren't in any immediate danger. We figured other people needed help more than we did. So I tried calling your father, but he didn't answer. That's when I called you."

Chet revved up the engine and steered the boat across the square. When we reached the other side, he killed the motor. Frank and I jumped onto the sidewalk and helped Aunt Trudy and Mom climb out of the boat.

"Good thing I wore my rain boots," said Aunt Trudy, stepping into an ankle-deep puddle. "I might look silly, but at least my feet are dry."

They climbed into the back of the Volkswagen to get out of the rain. Chet, Frank, and I were starting to pull the boat out of the water when we heard a scream.

"Help! Help! Somebody please help me!"

A woman's voice echoed across the town square.

I looked at Frank. "We have to help her," I said. "Mom! Aunt Trudy! Stay here while we go help that woman!"

We pushed the boat back into the water and

hopped inside. Chet revved up the motor and soon we were off, zooming toward an alley behind the bank.

"Help!"

Chet slowed down when we reached the entrance to the alley. "Where's the scream coming from?"

Frank pointed to a tiny store at the end of the narrow street. "Over there. Velma's Pawnshop."

Chet nodded and steered the boat closer to the tiny shop. It was just a ramshackle hut squashed between two taller buildings. The paint was peeling and the windows were smudged and packed with junk. A sign over the door spelled out the words VELMA'S PAWNSHOP: BUY, SELL, OR SWAP in curvy pink letters.

"Help me! Someone!"

The high-pitched voice came from somewhere inside the shop. Chet stopped the boat next to the doorway. Peering inside, we spotted a short, middle-aged woman with red hair, standing on top of a checkout counter.

"We're coming, ma'am," I said.

"Thank goodness!" she exclaimed. "I thought I'd never get out of here."

Frank and I hopped out of the boat, plunging feetfirst into the hip-deep water. Merchandise from the store floated all around us: old guitars, plastic ducks, leather coats, empty vases, oil paintings, jewelry boxes, you name it.

We made our way to the counter, then grasped each other's arms to make a human chair. "Your chariot awaits," said Frank.

Velma carefully lowered herself into our arms, and we carried her back to the boat. Chet reached down to help her climb aboard. Then my brother and I crawled into the boat.

"Okay, let's go, Chet," I said.

Our friend grabbed the handle of the outboard motor and started to go—but something made him suddenly stop.

"Look!" he said, pointing to the entrance of the shop.

Frank and I looked down and saw an electronic device floating through the doorway.

"That's my Zbox!" Chet exclaimed. "She's selling my stolen Zbox!"

"Wait a minute," said Frank. "How do you know it's yours?"

"See the sticker on the side?" said Chet. "I labeled it with my name. That's my Zbox!"

Frank and I turned around and stared at Velma. There was no mistaking the look on her face.

It was the look of guilt.

Chet leaned forward and pointed at Velma. "Where did you get that Zbox?" he asked her.

The woman shrugged her shoulders and glanced around nervously. "I—I don't remember."

I squatted down in front of her. "It's important," I said. "We need to know where you got that Zbox."

"S-someone sold it to me," she stuttered.

"Who?" I asked.

"I don't remember."

"Tell us. Who?"

Velma didn't answer me. Instead, she grabbed her left arm, then her chest, and started gasping for air. Her eyes rolled upward, lids fluttering. And then she fainted.

We stared down in shock, unsure what to do.

Velma Carter was either faking it—or she was having a heart attack.

SUSPECT PROFILE

Name: Velma Carter

Hometown: Jersey City, NJ

Physical description: 40 years old, 4'11", 125 lbs., red hair, pale skin, wears funky vintage clothing.

Occupation: Owner of Velma's Pawnshop

Background: Born in poor neighborhood of Jersey City, flunked out of school, arrested for shoplifting and fraud, served time in jail, moved to Bayport, and started up successful pawnshop.

Suspicious behavior: Tried to sell stolen goods.

Suspected of: Working with burglars to make profit on "hot" merchandise.

Possible motive: Easy money.

8.

Life Savers

Velma's body went limp.

Joe and I jumped up to catch her as she slumped over sideways. Reaching down, I grabbed her wrist and tried to find a pulse.

"Her heart's still beating," I said.

Joe put a finger under her nose. "And she's still breathing."

"We should do CPR," I said, rolling her onto her back. Joe tilted Velma's head backward to give her mouth-to-mouth resuscitation. But he never got the chance.

"Hold on, boys! We're coming!"

A small rescue boat zoomed toward us down the flooded alley, emergency lights flashing red

80

and yellow. It pulled up next to us, and two men hopped inside the motorboat.

It was Wilson and Grady, the two guys who'd rescued us at the docks.

"We'll take it from here," said Wilson, the short, stocky one.

Joe and I stepped aside to let the rescue workers do their job. The two former football players hunched down as if they were in a huddle. But when Grady started applying pressure to her chest, Velma opened her eyes—and screamed.

"Wait! No! Stop!"

She raised her arms and pushed them away.

"Calm down, lady," said Wilson. "We're here to help you."

"Yeah, relax," said Grady, holding her down.

Finally, Velma stopped struggling. Taking a deep breath, she stared up at the rescue workers and cleared her throat. "Okay, I feel better," she told them. "I must have fainted. You can let me up now."

"No, ma'am," said Wilson. "You're too weak. Grady and I will lift you onto our boat and take you to the medical center."

"I'm fine," Velma snapped. "I don't need a doctor."

"Sorry, but it's standard procedure," said Grady, picking her up in his brawny arms. "We just want to make sure you're okay."

"No! I don't want to go!"

Wilson and Grady ignored her protests as they placed her into their rescue boat.

"Will you boys be able to get back to dry land?" Grady asked us.

"No problem," said Chet, revving up the motor.

The two rescue workers waved good-bye, then zoomed off down the flooded street. As soon as they were gone, Chet pulled his Zbox out of the water and pointed at Velma's Pawnshop.

"What a weirdo," he said. "Why was she so upset about going to the medical center?"

"Maybe she's afraid," I said. "Someone might ask her what she was doing in her shop during a hurricane."

"Well, she's definitely up to no good," said Chet. "It turns out the rumors were true."

"What rumors?" asked Joe.

"A kid at school told me that Velma served time in prison. She's a common thief. And now here's the proof." Chet held up his Zbox.

Joe sighed. "I wish we could have asked her more questions."

"Me too," I said.

"At least I got my Zbox back," said Chet. "I just hope it still works."

I glanced down at the box, still dripping wet. The chances were slim.

Mom and Aunt Trudy were worried sick by the time we returned with the motorboat. We assured them we were okay and told them about Velma and the rescue team. Then we drove Chet to his house, unhooked the boat trailer, and went home to watch—what else?—the Weather Network.

"Hurricane Irene has caused record-breaking damage here in the Northeast," Johnny Thunder reported. "The storm wall in Bayport was breached, but an emergency crew has managed to patch the hole."

Then the pompous weatherman went on to describe these latest series of hurricanes as the worst in local history, comparing them to the disasters that typically hit the Gulf Coast. He called this "Our Summer of Storms" and used flashy computer graphics to back up his claims.

"Enough of this," Joe said, grabbing the remote.

He changed the channel to a local news station. An anchorman was talking about Hurricane Irene. "I can't take any more," said Joe, turning down the volume.

Seconds later, Wilson and Grady appeared on the screen. Live video footage showed the rescuers saving a family from a rooftop.

"Turn it up," I said.

Joe adjusted the volume and listened.

"Emergency rescue teams are extremely busy today," said the anchorman. "Many families did not evacuate their homes due to recent burglaries in the area. Most of those break-ins occurred after the false warning about Hurricane Ivy. Since then, residents have been very concerned about leaving their homes."

"I wonder if any houses were robbed today," said Joe.

"Shhh. Listen."

The anchorman continued. "The local police have received no reports of burglaries so far today. But it may be too early to tell. We'll keep you posted with any late-breaking news."

Then the anchorman turned the program over to a fuzzy-haired critic to review a new dinner theater production of *Grease*.

Joe turned off the TV and looked at me as we headed upstairs. "Maybe we should be out there. Someone could be robbing houses this very minute."

I stretched and yawned. "It's almost bedtime,

and half the town is knee-deep in water. Nobody wants a soggy Zbox."

"Nobody except Chet."

The next morning I was woken up by something really annoying. No, not Playback. It was my cell phone, ringing so loudly that I bolted out of bed and flipped on my phone.

"Hello?"

"Are you awake?"

"Now I am. Who is this?"

"It's Chet."

"What do you want, Chet?" I asked groggily.

"I'm heading down to the police station to tell them about finding my Zbox at Velma's Pawn-shop. I just wondered if you and Joe want to come along."

I couldn't tell Chet that my brother and I were already working on the case. So I said, "Sure. We'll join you. Where? When?"

"I'm standing in your yard right now."

I walked to the window and peeked outside. Chet stood below me, staring up and waving wildly.

"Sometimes you scare me, Chet."

I hung up the phone and went to wake up Joe. A few minutes later we were both dressed and out the door. Chet had borrowed his dad's car, so we hopped in and took off.

"Hey! Check out the town square," said Chet.

As we drove along the perimeter, we could see that most of yesterday's flooding had drained away. There were still a few monster puddles here and there, but at least it didn't look like a lake anymore.

Chet pulled his dad's car into the small parking lot in front of the police station. We got out, went inside, and walked up to the main desk.

"Hello, sir," said Chet, smiling at the heavyset receptionist. "I have some new information about the burglary I reported last week. Could I speak to one of the officers on the case?"

The receptionist let out a loud sigh and picked up a phone. "Hello, Lenny? I got a kid out here who thinks he knows something about the burglars. Can you take care of this?"

A few minutes later, two young officers strolled out to greet us. One was dark-haired, the other blond—and neither one of them was smiling.

"I'm Officer Welch," said the blond one. "And this is Officer Warner."

"I'm Frank, this is Joe—and Chet," I said, pushing him forward a little.

The darker one nodded grimly, looked at Chet, and said, "So whaddya got for us, kid?"

Chet cleared his throat a few times. Then he told them about finding his stolen Zbox at Velma's Pawnshop.

The two policemen looked at each other and shrugged. "It doesn't prove anything," said Officer Welch. "The burglar probably sold it to her." He shrugged again and turned to walk away.

"Wait," I said, shocked by their lack of interest. "Shouldn't you guys follow up on it? Ask Velma where she got it?"

Welch stopped and sighed. "Look, kid. Don't tell us how to do our job. We have a lot on our minds right now."

"Yeah," said his partner. "Thanks to this hurricane, we're pretty tied up. And your Zbox is pretty low on our to-do list."

Chet's mouth dropped open. "But—"

"We'll get back to you if there are any breakthroughs in the case."

Then Welch and Warner strolled off, slamming a big steel door behind them.

Joe shook his head. "They have to be the worst detectives on the force."

I had to agree. "We'll have to ask Dad about those two."

We walked out of the lobby and back to the car. Chet complained every step of the way.

"I can't believe what just happened in there," he said. "You would think they'd be happy about getting a lead in the case. But no, they just wanted to get rid of us."

"They must be overworked," I said, even though I didn't really believe what I was saying.

Chet opened the car door. "Now what, guys? Want to hang out, see a movie or something?"

"No, thanks, Chet," I said. "Joe and I need to get something at the store. You go on without us. We can walk home."

"We can?" said Joe.

I kicked his foot. "We promised Aunt Trudy. Remember, Joe?"

"Oh. Oh, yeah."

Chet seemed a little disappointed and tried to change our minds. Eventually he gave up, then started the car and drove off.

Joe looked at me. "Okay, what's up, bro? What do we need to get from the store?"

"Velma's confession," I said.

"Really? You think she's guilty?"

"I think she knows who sold her the Zbox. And I think we can get her to talk."

"How?" he asked.

"We can threaten to turn her in to the cops for selling stolen merchandise."

"But the cops don't seem to care."

"No, they don't," I said. "But Velma doesn't know that. And I bet she's not anxious to go back to prison."

I knew it was good idea—but Joe didn't say anything.

(He hates it when I'm right.)

The sun broke through the clouds as we crossed the town square. Even though the water had drained from the streets, the buildings were badly stained from all the flooding.

"What a mess," I said. "I hope the town is forming some sort of cleanup committee."

"We should volunteer to help."

"Good idea, Joe," I said, slapping his shoulder. "Thanks, man."

Joe took a deep breath.

"Yours is a good idea too, Frank," he said. "Getting Velma to talk. It's brilliant."

I raised my chin. "Yes, I know."

Joe pushed me into a puddle.

"I'll get you for that!"

I started chasing him across the square until we reached the alley. Then we stopped in our tracks.

"Dude! Check it out," said Joe.

The whole alley was littered with waterlogged merchandise from Velma's Pawnshop.

"I guess she hasn't come back yet," said Joe.

"Or maybe she left town before people started asking questions."

Without another word, we stepped into the alley and approached the little store.

The door was wide open.

Slowly we walked inside—and gasped at what we saw.

Velma Carter was lying on the floor, clutching her throat. Her chest heaved up and down. Her eyes rolled around in their sockets.

Joe and I rushed to her side.

With a stiff, trembling hand, Velma reached up toward us.

Then she uttered one simple word.

"Poison."

9.

Death in a Bottle

Poison?

I stared down at Velma, stunned and helpless.

"What happened?" I asked her.

She looked at me with pain in her eyes and nodded at a half-empty soda bottle on the floor.

Someone put poison in her soda.

I reached for the bottle, but Frank stopped me. "Don't touch it, Joe! There might be fingerprints on it!"

Then he pulled out his cell phone and dialed 911. "We need an ambulance at Velma's Pawnshop on Southside Alley," he told the operator. "Velma's been poisoned."

Velma grabbed my hand and squeezed.

"Who did this to you?" I asked her.

She raised her head and tried to speak. I leaned in closer, tilting my ear toward her mouth.

"W . . ."

That's all I heard—a W sound.

Then she closed her eyes and slumped back.

No!

I was starting to check her pulse when someone yelled from the doorway.

"Step aside, boys!"

It was Officer Welch and his partner, Officer Warner. They rushed into the tiny shop, practically knocking Frank and me to the floor. Warner, the dark-haired one, knelt down over Velma's body. Welch picked up the soda bottle.

He's touching the evidence.

I was ready to point out his faulty police work when an ambulance came roaring down the alley. Lights flashing and siren blaring, it screeched to a stop in front of the store. Two paramedics jumped out and rushed inside.

"Hurry," I said. "We think she's been poisoned."

Officer Warner stood up to let the paramedics examine the body. Then he turned and stared at Frank and me.

"What were you boys doing here?" he asked.

"We wanted to ask Velma about the stolen Zbox," I said without hesitation.

Frank smacked my arm.

Officer Warner frowned. "That's our job, boys."

"Really?" I said. "It seems to me that you and your partner aren't very interested in the case."

Warner's face turned red. "Look here," he said, scowling. "I understand that your father used to be some big-time detective back in New York. But this is Bayport, and it's our beat now. So butt out."

I started to protest, but Frank grabbed my arm.

Then Officer Welch stepped in. "Okay, enough is enough. You boys should go home now," he said. "Leave the police work to the professionals."

Frank pushed me toward the door and into the alley. As we started to go, one of the paramedics stood up over Velma's body and announced something to the officers, who turned to us.

"Too late," he said. "She's dead."

When we got home, we told our father everything that had happened at the police station and Velma's Pawnshop. He leaned back in his office chair and listened carefully.

"What were the names of the two officers?" he asked.

"Welch and Warner," I told him.

Dad made a face and rolled his eyes. "Oh, those guys. They're fresh out of the police academy, and nobody on the force likes them."

"Do you think they could be involved?" asked Frank.

Dad shrugged. "I don't know. I doubt it. They're just a couple of jerks who think they know everything."

We talked a little more about Velma and the stolen Zbox. Dad thought she probably knew the merchandise was stolen—and that's why she was silenced. The burglars were afraid she would identify them to the police.

"Nobody likes a squealer," said Dad. "Especially lowlife criminals who have everything to lose if the squealer talks."

We thanked Dad and headed upstairs to Frank's bedroom. Playback greeted us with a loud squawk. I fed him a parrot treat and flopped down onto Frank's bed.

"I want to check my e-mail," he said, turning on the computer.

I stared up at the ceiling. "You know what, Frank? I think we should add Welch and Warner to our suspect list."

My brother sighed. "But they're cops, Joe.

What are the chances that they're burglars, too?"

I sat up. "You've never heard the expression 'good cop, bad cop'? Those two are definitely bad cops."

Frank stared blankly at the screen as the computer warmed up. "Well, I agree that they're bad detectives. But that doesn't prove anything."

"No, but I didn't tell you what Velma whispered right before she died."

Frank turned away from the screen and looked at me. "What?"

"W . . ."

Frank seemed confused. "Huh?"

"She started to say a word that began with the letter W," I explained. "As in Welch or Warner."

Frank thought about it. "Maybe she was trying to say something like 'Why me?' or 'What happened?'"

"Maybe," I said. "But I still think those guys should go on our suspect list. We know there's more than one burglar because of the voices we heard at Chet's house."

Frank turned back to the computer and logged on to check his e-mail. He was greeted by the cheerful sound of *"You've got mail!"* Clicking the mouse, he leaned forward and read the new message.

"Joe."

"What?"

"Come here. You've got to read this."

I stood up and walked to the desk. Leaning over Frank's shoulder, I read the e-mail on the screen.

```
* * * * * * * * * * * * * * * * * * * * * * *
* * I N C O M I N G   T R A N S M I S S I O N * *
* * * * * * * * * * * * * * * * * * * * * * *
To: hardy1@americalink.com
From: WorstNightmare@AddressUnknown
Subject: Warning
Message: Stay away from Velma's Pawnshop—or
you'll be sorry. This is your last warning. W.
* * * * * * * * * * * * * * * * * * * * * * *
```

I reread the message a few more times, then looked down at Frank.

"It's signed W. See? Now do you believe that Welch and Warner are guilty?"

Frank gazed at the screen. "It could also stand for WorstNightmare@AddressUnknown."

I threw my hands into the air. "Give me a break, Frank. Those cops wanted us out of that pawnshop as soon as they laid eyes on us."

Frank still wasn't convinced. "It's a crime scene, Joe. That's what the police do—they make every-

SUSPECT PROFILE

Name: John Welch

Hometown: Eastwood

Physical description: 25 years old, 6'1", 195 lbs., blond hair and freckles, muscular build.

Occupation: Police officer

Background: He was the school troublemaker, always pulling pranks to get attention, best friends with Todd Warner. They went to the police academy together—and barely graduated.

Suspicious behavior: Refused to follow a lead in the burglary case, last name begins with W.

Suspected of: Burglarizing homes in the Bayport area.

Possible motive: Pulling off the ultimate prank.

one leave the crime scene so no one tampers with the evidence."

I rolled my eyes. "Yeah, but how did they get there so fast? Welch and Warner showed up at the shop barely two minutes after you called 911."

Frank took a deep breath. I could see the wheels

SUSPECT PROFILE

__Name:__ Todd Warner

__Hometown:__ Eastwood

__Physical description:__ 26 years old, 5'9", 200 lbs., dark hair and stubble, stocky build.

__Occupation:__ Police officer

__Background:__ He was the school bully, always picking fights to prove himself, ashamed of growing up poor, joined Bayport police force with his buddy John Welch—and made a lot of enemies.

__Suspicious behavior:__ Displayed anger when questioned about the burglary case, last name also begins with W.

__Suspected of:__ Burglarizing homes in the Bayport area.

__Possible motive:__ Looking for easy money—to make up for a hard life.

turning in his head. Finally he looked up at me and said, "Okay, Joe. Add them to our list."

The more I thought about it, the more it made sense. As local police officers, Welch and Warner would know which neighborhoods were being evacuated. They helped people on the way to the emergency evacuation center at the high school. Nobody would ever suspect them.

Nobody except me.

I sat down again on Frank's bed. Playback flew across the room and landed on the headboard behind me. "What do you think, Playback?" I said. "Are they guilty?"

The parrot looked at me and flapped his wings. "Guilty! Guilty! Guilty!"

"See?" I said to Frank. "Even Playback agrees with me."

My brother leaned back in his chair, chewing on a pen. "I just wish we had proof."

"I know where we can get it."

"Where?"

"Velma's Pawnshop."

Frank stopped chewing.

"Think about it," I continued. "The e-mail told us to stay away from the pawnshop. That's where we'll find our proof."

"But it's a crime scene, Joe. The police probably sealed it off."

"So?"

"So how do we get in?"

"Simple," I said. "We break in. Tonight. At midnight."

He gave me a look, which I knew all too well: We're supposed to enforce the law, not *break* the law.

"Someone has to make sure justice is served, right?" I reminded him.

He knew I had a point.

We waited until Mom, Dad, and Aunt Trudy went to bed. Then we tiptoed downstairs, trying not to disturb Playback, who was fast asleep in his covered cage in the living room. When we got outside, I started walking toward our motorcycles, but Frank stopped me.

"The engines are too loud," he whispered. "Let's ride our bikes."

I wasn't thrilled with the idea. My ten-speed was a little rusty—and permanently stuck in fourth gear. But hey, it still worked, so I followed Frank to the garage.

"Okay," I said. "Let's do this."

Ten minutes later we were zipping along silently on our bikes, zooming across the town square. A police car was circling the fountain, so we ducked behind a van and hunched down until it passed. Then we rode quickly and quietly to Southside Alley.

Velma's Pawnshop was totally dark. Yellow ribbons of police tape—labeled CRIME SCENE: DO NOT CROSS—were stretched across the doorway.

But that wasn't going to stop Frank and me.

We hid our bikes behind a small Dumpster and walked to the front of the store. In the dim light of the streetlamp, I could see that the police had secured the door with a heavy steel bolt and padlock.

"Looks like we're locked out," I said.

Frank squinted his eyes. "No. Check it out. The lock's been broken."

I stepped into the shadowed doorway and examined the padlock. It had been cut with a heavy-duty bolt cutter.

"Someone's already been here," I said.

Frank didn't say anything. Removing the padlock, he grabbed the handle and pushed the door open. Then, ducking down, we slipped beneath the yellow police tape.

Inside, the shop was pitch-black. "I can't see a thing," I said.

"That's okay. I came prepared," said Frank. He pulled a small LCD flashlight out of his back pocket, gave it a few shakes, and turned it on.

"Frank! Look over there!"

He pointed the beam at the checkout counter. The cash register was open, the drawer empty. The counter was totally covered with papers and receipts that spilled onto the floor.

"Somebody was looking for something," Frank whispered.

"Do you think they found what they were looking for?"

Frank shrugged. I went behind the counter and started poking around, while my brother examined the rest of the store. Feeling my way in the darkness, I reached beneath the counter and ran my fingers across the wood until—

"Hey. What's this?"

Frank turned around, flashing the light in my direction. I showed him a secret drawer under the counter. After I jiggled it a few times, the drawer popped open. Then I reached inside and pulled out a large black ledger.

"It's Velma's record book," I said, flipping through the pages.

"Let me see." Frank shone the flashlight over the rumpled, handwritten pages. "It's full of shipments, and dates, and deliveries—and clients."

"So we can see who sold her Chet's Zbox," I said.

"There's just one problem." Frank sighed. "All the ink is smudged. The floodwater must have gotten to it."

"Can you make out any names?"

Frank leaned over and studied the book carefully, examining page after page. "I can't read any names," he said. "But wait—here's a shipment of electronics dated last week, right after the fake hurricane."

I moved closer. "Who sold it to her?"

"I can't read the name," said Frank. "But there's a pickup address."

"Where is it?"

My brother looked at me, his eyes glowing from the flashlight. When he told me the address, I started to laugh—because it sounded like something out of a bad horror movie.

"Warehouse Thirteen."

10.

Warehouse 13

Joe and I decided to take the water-stained ledger with us—for evidence. As we left the pawnshop, I made sure to replace the broken padlock and wipe off my fingerprints. Then we walked to our bikes hidden behind the Dumpster.

"Let's go check out Warehouse Thirteen," said Joe.

"Two break-ins in one night? Sure. Why not?"

We hopped on our bikes and started riding toward the docks near the bay. The moon was full and bright in the night sky. We could see the old warehouses that sat on the piers over the water. Some of them had been damaged by the recent storm, but most were in pretty good shape.

"Four, five, six." I counted the warehouses as we rode our bikes down the boardwalk.

Finally we reached Warehouse 13.

"Here it is," I said, stopping my bike and pointing at a small sign.

"Looks spooky," said Joe.

"Are you scared?"

"Are you kidding? I'm anxious to catch these creeps."

We jumped off our bikes and stashed them in the shadows beneath the boardwalk. Then we started walking down the pier toward the warehouse entrance.

"I just thought of something," I said. "When Velma was dying, she might have been trying to say 'Warehouse Thirteen,' not the burglar's name. It starts with a W."

"You just don't want to believe that cops could be criminals."

"No. I just don't want to believe that you could solve a crime before I did."

"Get over it, Frank."

We had a little chuckle, then grew quiet as we approached the warehouse. A bare lightbulb hung down over a huge doorway, casting an eerie glow across the weathered planks of the pier. The waves from the bay lapped gently against the dock, and somewhere in the distance a foghorn let out a long, lonely wail.

"*Now* are you scared?" I asked Joe.

"No, but I'm afraid we won't be able to get into this warehouse."

He pointed at the massive iron deadbolt on the door. The sliding bolt was held in place with a solid steel padlock that must have been the size of my fist.

"I'm disappointed, Joe," I said. "You're going to let a little thing like that stop you?"

"Well, I'm saving up my superhuman strength for something more challenging." He flexed his bicep.

I rolled my eyes and pushed him off balance.

"Come on, Superdork," I said, turning around. "Let's see if we can find another way to get inside."

We walked along the perimeter of the warehouse until we reached the end of the pier. At the corner of the building, hidden in shadows, was a huge stack of empty wooden crates. I stopped and pointed toward the roof.

"Look. There's a little window up there. Probably for air circulation."

Joe gazed up and squinted. "It's pretty high, Frank."

"That shouldn't be a problem for Superdork."

Joe ignored me. "We can stack these crates under the window and climb up to it," he said.

"Sounds like a good plan, hero," I said. "So what are you waiting for?"

"I'm waiting for you to knock it off and help me."

I stopped teasing him and started pushing crates across the pier. The boxes were empty, so they weren't too heavy. But they were so big and bulky that it took both of us to lift them up and stack them.

It took about five minutes to build a small tower alongside the building. Then Joe and I climbed to the top and pulled ourselves up to the windowsill.

We peeked inside.

The warehouse was too dark to see anything. I pulled out my LCD flashlight, gave it a few shakes, and aimed the beam inside. Just beneath the window, we saw a tall metal shelving unit.

"Excellent," I said. "Go on, Joe. Climb down."

"Why do I have to go first?"

"Because you're Super—"

"Frank."

"Okay. I'll stop. Go ahead. I'll light the way for you."

Taking a deep breath, Joe lowered his feet onto the top shelf. Then he swung his legs over the side and started climbing down. A few seconds later, his feet hit the floor.

"Okay. I made it," he whispered to me. "Toss me the flashlight."

I dropped it down, then lowered myself onto the steel unit, using each shelf like the rung of a ladder. As I slowly descended, I noticed all sorts of stuff sitting on the shelves—flat-screen TVs, stereo equipment, silver tea sets, jewelry, and other valuable items.

We're in the burglar's lair.

I hopped to the floor and looked around. Joe used the flashlight to scan the building, illuminating row after row of stolen goods. We seemed to be standing on a huge balcony that overlooked the main floor of the warehouse. Walking to the edge, Joe shone the flashlight downward.

"Dude! Look at all that junk!"

The lower level was filled with a lot of the same things that were stored up in the balcony—except all of it was obviously ruined by floodwater.

"I'll bet the burglars were pretty bummed when they saw all this damage," I said.

Joe glanced behind us. "That's probably why they're storing stuff up here now."

He turned around and examined a few large wooden crates. Lifting a lid, he peered inside—and screamed.

"Auuughh!"

I jumped. "What is it, Joe?"

"Nothing," he said, laughing. "It's empty. I'm just messing with you, Frank. You should have seen the look on your face! You were scared silly!"

"I was not."

Joe started to say something else, and then I heard a sound that really *did* scare me.

"Joe! Shhh! What's that?"

He listened. "What's what?"

"That."

From the other side of the warehouse, on the lower level, came the faint sound of keys jingling outside the door—and the scraping rattle of a sliding metal bolt.

"Someone's coming," I whispered. "Quick, hide."

Joe lifted the lid of the empty crate and jumped inside. I wasn't sure if there was enough room in there for both of us, but I didn't have a choice.

Somebody opened the warehouse door.

I quickly crawled into the crate next to Joe and lowered the lid over our heads. My heart felt like it was pounding double-time. But then I realized that half of the heartbeats belonged to Joe, who was squashed up against me.

He elbowed me in the ribs, and I elbowed him right back. But we both froze when we heard the two voices on the lower level.

"You're crazy, man."

"No, I'm not. I swear I heard someone scream. Right before you opened the door."

"It was just the waves hitting the dock."

One of them flicked a switch. A row of fluorescent lights flickered on, beaming down from the ceiling and penetrating the boards of the crate.

"Man! Look at all this stuff!" said one of the voices. "It's ruined."

"I told you to store everything on the balcony. If you had listened to me in the first place, we wouldn't have to throw this junk away."

"Sorry, man."

"It's money down the drain."

"I said I'm sorry."

I listened carefully, trying to identify the voices.

Who's talking? Welch and Warner? Johnny Thunder and Irwin Link?

I couldn't be sure. The warehouse had a bad echo, and the wooden crate we were hiding in distorted the sound even more.

I tried to listen closer.

For a while all I could hear were the sounds of shuffling footsteps and things being moved around. Then suddenly the two of them stopped working and started talking again.

"I'm worried," said one.

"About what?" said the other.

"Getting caught."

"Who's going to turn us in? Velma? She's history."

"I know. But now that she's out of the picture, how are we going to unload all this stuff?"

"Don't worry. I have a connection in Eastwood."

The mention of Eastwood caught my attention.

Johnny Thunder and Irwin Link work in Eastwood. Maybe they're partners in a larger crime ring.

I heard more shuffling around below us.

"Hey. Look at these."

"What?"

"The water didn't reach these oil paintings. They're still good."

"So take them up to the balcony."

"Okay."

A pair of heavy footsteps started coming up the stairs.

I felt Joe tense up next to me.

"Where should I put them?" the voice yelled down to his partner.

"They're pretty small. They should fit inside one of those empty crates."

Oh, no, I thought.

"Which empty crates?"

"There. On the edge of the balcony."

The footsteps started walking—straight toward us.

I sucked in my breath.

My heart began pounding, my stomach clenching into a tight ball. I braced myself for the worst.

You can take him, Frank, I told myself. *Just jump out and surprise him, like a jack-in-the-box.*

I flexed my leg muscles and clenched my fists. Joe must have had the same idea, because he was doing it too.

The footsteps stopped right in front of us.

"These crates here?" the voice yelled down.

"Yeah."

A hand reached down and flipped open the lid.

Surprise!

Nothing happened.

Joe and I didn't jump up and attack—because the man opened the crate *next* to ours instead.

Ha!

With a loud grunt, he shoved the paintings inside the box and slammed the lid. Then he headed back to the steps and went downstairs.

Joe and I let out sighs of relief—very *quiet* sighs, of course.

Man, that was close.

We listened to the footsteps cross the lower level.

"What are you doing?"

"Counting up how much we lost because of the flooding."

"Is it a lot?"

"Yeah, almost half of everything we stole."

"What are we going to do?"

"What do you mean, what are we going to do? We're going to steal *more* stuff, that's what we're going to do."

"Oh."

Then there was more shuffling and the echoing sound of footsteps, followed by the clank of a bolt and the click of a light switch.

The warehouse was plunged into darkness again.

One of them opened the huge steel door.

"So how are we going to steal more stuff? Do you have another plan?"

"Who needs another plan?"

"You mean—?"

"Yeah. We'll just make up another fake hurricane."

11.
Running for Shelter

The next morning Frank woke me up by tossing an old pair of paint-covered overalls onto my pillow.

"Get up! Get dressed! Get moving!"

I pushed one of the denim straps off my face and groaned. "Don't tell me Mom wants us to paint the house."

"No, but I thought you'd want to wear your old clothes today," said Frank. "I volunteered us for the hurricane cleanup committee."

Whistling cheerfully, he pulled up the window shades to fill the room with light.

He was so chipper about it that I wanted to smack him.

"I'm tired, Frank," I mumbled, pulling the overalls across my face. "Wake me up when it's over."

Frank walked over to the bed. "That's okay, Joe. You can just lay there and sleep all day while the poor victims of Hurricane Irene struggle to pick up the pieces of their lives."

"Thanks for the guilt trip."

"So? Are you going to help?"

"Yes, I'll help," I said, uncovering my face. "As long as I don't have to wear these stupid overalls."

"You can wear a tutu for all I care."

"Really? Can I borrow *yours*?"

Frank responded by lifting the mattress and flipping me onto the floor.

Twenty minutes later I was up and dressed and walking downtown. Frank kept talking about the burglars and thinking of ways to catch them.

"We could set up a motion-sensitive videocam outside their warehouse," he said. "Then we'd have visual evidence connecting those guys to the stolen goods."

"I'd rather catch them in the act," I said.

I gazed down the street at a long row of houses.

They look like sitting ducks at a shooting gallery, I thought. *Just waiting to be picked off one by one.*

"Did you watch the Weather Network this morning?" I asked Frank.

"Yeah. But there were no reports of another hurricane."

I kicked a pebble and sighed. "I guess we just have to wait for the burglars to strike again."

"Don't worry, Joe. The cleanup committee will keep us busy."

We turned the corner, walked to the town square—and were shocked by what we found there.

"Wow! Check it out!" I said. "Looks like everyone in Bayport showed up to help."

The town square was buzzing with activity. Men and women, young and old, were all pitching in—sweeping the garbage from the gutters, throwing tree branches into Dumpsters, scrubbing water stains off the buildings, and hosing down the sidewalks.

Frank smiled. "There sure are a lot of familiar faces here."

He was right.

Chet Morton and Iola were wiping down the park benches. Brian and Belinda Conrad were cleaning out the stone fountain. Dr. Melissa Robinson, our family doctor, scrubbed a dirty mailbox with a big sponge.

"Hi, boys!" she shouted to us.

Some of our teachers from school were there

too, like Mr. Mirabella, our gym teacher, and Mr. Brooks, the assistant principal. I spotted Grady, one of the rescue workers we'd met, helping Police Chief Collig push a rolling Dumpster across the street.

Even Aunt Trudy was there, handing out sandwiches.

"It's about time you got here," she said to us.

"Frank had a little trouble getting me out of bed," I said. "Could I have a sandwich?"

"Not until you do some work." She pointed to the sign-up desk at the end of the square and pushed me away from the sandwiches.

As we headed to the desk, I lowered my voice and said, "Just think, Frank. The burglars could be here right now."

"Unless they're robbing our houses while we work."

"Oh. I didn't think of that."

We walked up to the desk and asked a volunteer what we could do to help. The white-haired woman smiled and pointed at a huge lumpy mud puddle on the corner.

"Someone needs to clean that mess," she said sweetly. "The sewer drain backed up."

Great, I thought. *That's what I get for sleeping in and being the last to volunteer.*

The white-haired woman handed us two shovels and a large bucket. "Thanks a lot, boys."

We walked over to the murky puddle. I looked down, took a whiff, and made a face.

Frank laughed. "Aw, get over it, Joe. It's a dirty job, but someone has to do it."

"Yeah, but this really stinks."

Frank covered his nose. "I'm with you, bro."

We grabbed our shovels and went to work.

It turned out that we didn't have to worry about everyone's houses being robbed that day. According to the news, there were no more burglaries to report. And according to the Weather Network, no hurricanes, either.

Just to be sure, Frank and I watched the Weather Network every day—morning, noon, and night—waiting for Johnny Thunder to predict another phony hurricane.

But it never happened.

In fact, a whole week and a half went by without hurricane warnings, emergency evacuations, burglaries, or any criminal activity at all. Frank even went to the docks one night to hide a motion-sensitive videocam near the entrance of Warehouse 13, but the tapes were always blank. The burglars never came back.

Is that it? I thought. *Mission over?*

But then, one cloudy afternoon, it happened.

The Weather Network reported another hurricane.

We were sitting in the living room with our parents and Aunt Trudy when we heard the news.

"Hurricane Jason could be the worst storm we've ever seen," Johnny Thunder announced grimly. "At this very moment, Jason is gathering strength in the middle of the Atlantic Ocean. It's moving fast and gaining momentum, with winds up to one hundred thirty miles per hour. And yes, ladies and gentlemen, it's heading right for us."

Aunt Trudy stopped knitting. Mom and Dad dropped their newspapers and looked up at the TV.

Johnny Thunder continued. "If you live in the Bayport area—or anywhere near the coast—we strongly advise you to evacuate your homes immediately."

Aunt Trudy stood up from her chair.

"I repeat," said Johnny. "Evacuate your homes immediately. Hurricane Jason promises to be even more devastating than Irene, reaching a level of Category Four or Five. For your own safety, we urge you to go to the closest emergency shelter in your community."

Mom turned to Dad. "It sounds serious, Fen. Do you think we should we evacuate?"

"Of *course* we should evacuate," Aunt Trudy chimed in. "Johnny Thunder said it could be Category Four or Five."

"Johnny Thunder has been known to make mistakes, Gertrude," said my father.

"Gertrude?" I said, laughing. "Nobody ever calls you that, Aunt Trudy."

"Well, it *is* my name," she replied, a little annoyed.

"Then why does everyone call you Trudy?" I asked.

"It's a long story, *Joseph*," she said. "I'll tell you why later. Right now, we should get ready to evacuate."

Mom and Dad agreed.

"Go pack some extra underwear," Mom told us. "And take Playback to your room."

Playback heard his name and flapped his wings. Then he followed Frank and me upstairs.

"This way, birdbrain," my brother cooed to the parrot.

As fast as I could, I threw some clothes into my backpack, then went to Frank's room. He was sitting on his bed, listening to the hand-cranked emergency radio we got from the ATAC team.

"Any news?" I asked.

Frank frowned and shook his head. "Nobody except the Weather Network is reporting Hurricane Jason."

"Are you sure?"

Frank didn't answer me. Instead, he reached for the other "toy" we'd received from ATAC—a mini "weather tracker" device with satellite hookup. Fidgeting with the dials, he pulled up a weather map on the tiny screen and studied it carefully.

"The satellite shows some hurricane activity," he said, "but it's a lot farther away than Johnny Thunder told us."

"So you think . . . ?"

"Yeah. Hurricane Jason could be another fake."

I gazed across the room, wondering if my brother was right, and then I noticed Playback sitting calmly in his cage.

"He's not ruffling his feathers," I muttered.

"Huh?" said Frank.

"Aunt Trudy said Playback ruffles his feathers when a storm is coming. But look at him."

"That's one mellow bird," Frank agreed.

Just then, Mom shouted up to us from the bottom of the stairs. "Hurry up, guys! We're ready to go!"

"We're coming, Mom!" I yelled down.

Moving quickly, Frank and I stuffed the weather tracker and the emergency radio into our backpacks—along with the ultraslim inflatable life vests. Then we headed downstairs.

"We're going to take our motorcycles, Mom," said Frank, dashing to the front door.

"But wait, it's not safe," she said.

"Please, Mom," I pleaded. "It's not even raining."

She started to protest, but Dad butted in. "Go ahead, boys. We'll meet you at the evacuation center."

Frank and I turned and charged out of the house before Mom could veto Dad's decision. As we revved up our motorcycles, I asked my brother where we were going.

"We have to warn everyone," he answered. "The town of Bayport is about to be hit by burglars—not a hurricane."

He pulled out his cell phone and speed-dialed the Bayport Police Department. "Could I speak to Chief Collig, please?"

He paused for a second.

"Okay, thanks."

He turned off the phone and looked at me.

"Collig is at the evacuation center," he explained. "Let's go."

Not wasting any time, we took off down the street. We had to weave our motorcycles in and out of all the traffic caused by Johnny Thunder's warning.

Hundreds of people were evacuating their homes.

They were also leaving their houses at the mercy of rotten, thieving crooks.

We'll get those guys.

I leaned forward on my motorcycle and stayed close behind my brother.

In minutes we reached the high school parking lot. It was packed with cars and crowded with people. Men, women, and children stood in line, glancing nervously at the sky. Closer to the entrance sat two white ambulances, a van full of supplies, and four police cars.

Frank and I parked our motorcycles on the edge of the lot. Then we hopped off and started walking toward the entrance.

But when we saw the two policemen standing at the door, we froze in our tracks.

It was Officer Welch and Officer Warner.

"Well, well, well, look who it is," said Welch, swinging his nightstick. "Looking for shelter, boys?"

Warner scoffed. "Nah, they're looking for clues."

"Oh, I forgot. They think they're detectives."

Frank cleared his throat and stepped up in front of them. "We need to talk to Chief Collig."

Warner raised a dark eyebrow. "Why? Did you boys finally crack the case of the missing Zbox?"

He winked at his partner, and the two burst out laughing.

"Go to the back of the line like everyone else," said Welch, sneering.

"It's important," said Frank. "We have information."

"What kind of information?" asked Warner.

Frank paused. "It's about the hurricane. Please. Let me talk to the chief."

"What about the hurricane?" asked Welch. "Tell us, and we'll make sure Collig gets the message."

Frank bit his lip and didn't answer him.

Warner let out a sigh and glanced at his partner. "It looks like we got a pair of troublemakers here."

"Yeah," said Welch. "They're nothing like their father, that's for sure."

I couldn't take it any longer.

"Will you guys knock it off and listen?" I said, my voice rising with my anger. "We need to tell Chief Collig that the burglars are about to strike!"

"Oh, really?" said Welch with a smirk.

"Yes, really!" I went on. "There is no Hurricane

Jason. It's just a scam to get people to evacuate their homes!"

Suddenly I realized how loudly I was shouting. People around the door began to murmur and shift toward us.

"Did he just say Hurricane Jason is a scam?" asked one woman.

"Yeah, the burglars are going to strike," answered another.

Then everyone started talking at once.

Some people tried to push their way out of the auditorium. Others swarmed around us, asking questions.

"Now look what you did," Officer Welch snarled. "You're causing everyone to panic."

Warner looked at his partner. "I told you they were troublemakers."

Before I knew it, he grabbed me by the arm and squeezed hard.

Then he slapped a handcuff on my wrist.

"You're under arrest!"

FRANK

12.

Ruffled Feathers

When Officer Warner said, "You're under arrest," my first instinct was to run.

And that's exactly what I did.

Officer Welch whipped out his handcuffs and lunged for my wrist. But before he could grab me, I dropped to the ground and dove into the crowd.

Behind me, Joe did the exact same thing—except in his case, he had to do it with a pair of handcuffs dangling and jangling from his left wrist.

"Don't let them get away!" shouted Officer Welch.

He yelled into the crowd and tried to chase after us. Legs and feet shuffled back and forth in front of me as I crawled away from the auditorium entrance.

"Stop in the name of the law!"

Yeah, right.

I kept on crawling—full steam ahead—knocking into knees, thwacking thighs, squashing toes, even shimmying through the shins of a bowlegged lady.

Finally I reached the edge of the crowd. Jumping to my feet, I glanced back to see if Joe was still behind me.

He was.

Way to go, Joe!

His blond head popped out from beneath a woman's dress. Then he scrambled to his feet and swatted my arm, accidentally scraping me with the handcuffs.

"Ouch! That hurt!" I yelped.

"Stop whining! Start running!" he gasped.

I looked back. Welch and Warner were fighting their way through the crowd—but they could still see us. Joe and I quickly ducked down behind a parked car and made our way across the lot.

A minute later we hopped onto our motorcycles and hit the road.

We made it.

Now, don't get me wrong.

Resisting arrest is a serious offense, and I don't recommend it. In fact, arguing with a police officer will only get you into more trouble than you're already in.

But I look at it this way: Joe and I were on an undercover mission for American Teens Against Crime, which works directly with the local police chief. The arresting officers, Welch and Warner, were at the top of our suspect list. And if Joe and I hadn't run away, more serious crimes would be committed—crimes we were trying to stop.

It was all part of our mission. We were trying to *uphold* the law, not *escape* it.

Okay?

I just needed to get that off my chest before going on with the story.

As soon as we made our "getaway," Joe and I went straight home. In spite of the fact that we were "wanted criminals," it didn't seem necessary to run and hide. Also, I had to use the bathroom.

"But what if Welch and Warner come here looking for us?" asked Joe, climbing off his motorcycle.

I took off my helmet. "If Welch and Warner are innocent, they won't bother chasing a couple of kids with a crazy theory about Hurricane Jason. They'll be too busy at the evacuation center."

"Yeah, but what if they're guilty?"

"Then they'll come after us—and expose themselves as the burglars. Case closed."

"Or *coffin* closed, if they try to kill us."

"Don't worry. I'll protect you, Joe."

"As if."

I ran inside to use the bathroom while Joe grabbed a hacksaw from the garage. Then we headed to my room, tossing our backpacks on the bed and getting down to business.

"I'll check the news." I pulled the emergency radio out of my backpack and gave it a few cranks.

"I'll catch a few Zs," said Joe.

By "Zs" he meant sawing at his handcuff.

"Hey! Don't do that here. You'll mess up my bedspread."

He stopped and rolled his eyes. Moving to the window, he plopped down on the sill and started sawing again.

"Thank you, Joe."

"You're welcome, Martha Stewart."

Ignoring him, I turned on the radio and scanned the dial. After a few tries, I found a good news channel.

"And now for our local weather," said the announcer.

I turned up the volume.

"It has just been confirmed that the recent

reports of Hurricane Jason are completely false. National weather authorities firmly deny the existence of a Hurricane Jason. The first—and only—reports have come from Johnny Thunder of the Weather Network, the same anchorman who predicted a nonexistent hurricane named Ivy just a few weeks ago."

I looked at Joe to see his reaction—but he was too busy sawing the handcuff. The sound was so loud I could barely hear the radio.

"Joe! Quiet! I want to hear this!"

He stopped sawing.

"Thousands of residents in the Bayport area have evacuated their homes," the newsman continued. "But even though Hurricane Jason doesn't exist, local authorities are urging residents to stay in the evacuation centers because—"

A crackle of static blared from the radio, garbling the newsman's voice.

"Great. Now I lost the reception."

I fidgeted with the knobs a little bit, but no luck. Joe finished sawing off his handcuff, then sat back and rubbed his wrist.

"Frank."

"Shhh. I think I'm getting something."

"Frank."

I started losing my patience. "What?"

"Look at Playback."

I turned my head and gazed at the parrot cage in the corner. "What?" I asked again.

"He's ruffling his feathers."

Joe was right.

Playback's feathers were standing on end, ruffling back and forth. With a loud squawk, he twitched and scratched his perch.

"You know what that means, don't you?" said Joe. "A storm is coming."

"According to Aunt Trudy," I pointed out. "But it can't be Hurricane Jason. The man on the radio said it was a false alarm."

Joe turned his head toward the window. "So how do you explain this?"

I looked over.

It was raining outside—and raining hard.

That's weird.

I got up and walked to the window. Raindrops pelted the glass. Trees swayed back and forth as a heavy wind picked up speed.

"Man! Look at that storm!" Joe gasped.

"Yeah, it's pretty major," I said. "But it's not a hurricane."

"Oh, no? Then what is it?"

"I don't know. Just your typical summer storm."

"Oh, yeah? Then why did 'your typical summer

storm' just knock over our mailbox?"

I leaned closer to the window and peered down at the front yard. The mailbox was lying flat on the ground, while tree branches and garbage rolled past it.

Suddenly I realized how dark it was.

Glancing at the clock radio on my nightstand, I saw that it was only three in the afternoon—but inside it was as dark as midnight.

"I'm going to turn on the light." I walked across the room and flipped the switch.

"Frank! Turn it off! Quick!"

I snapped off the light. "Why? What's up?"

"Come here and take a look," said Joe.

Crouching down next to my brother, I gazed out the window at the storm. But all I could see was our neighbors' houses—being pummeled with rain and wind.

"What am I looking for, Joe?"

"The moving van."

I squinted my eyes. "What moving van?"

Joe pointed at the Rubins' house across the street. "See? Right there. It's parked on the driveway next to the house."

I pressed my nose to the rain-streaked windowpane and looked again. It was hard to see anything in all that rain. But finally I spotted it beneath the trees—a large black van parked just a few feet away from the Rubins' house. Its rear door was slid open—and the back was filled with TV sets, computers, and other stuff.

Then I saw them.

The burglars.

Two men dressed in dark, hooded Windbreakers were hauling a flat-screen TV from the house and loading it into the back of the van.

"There they are!" I gasped.

Joe leaned over me. "Can you see who they are?"

"No, they're wearing hoods. Try the binoculars."

Joe reached for the binoculars on my desk and peered through them out the window.

"Well?" I asked.

"I still can't see their faces," he said.

I stood up. "Come on. Let's get these guys."

Moving quickly, we pulled the life vests out of our backpacks, put them on, and slipped into our Windbreakers. Before leaving the room, I grabbed the emergency radio and tucked it into the pocket of my jacket.

"Hurry!" said Joe. "We can't let them get away this time!"

"I'm right behind you, bro."

In a flash we were down the stairs and heading for the front door.

"Joe, wait," I said. "They might see us."

"You're right. We'll go out the back."

We turned and dashed through the kitchen. Joe flung open the door—and was almost knocked over by a blast of wind and rain.

Joe braced himself and howled, "Are you *sure* this isn't a hurricane?"

"Get moving."

I pushed him outside and stepped onto the porch, closing the door behind me. We flipped up the hoods of our Windbreakers and ducked down. Then we made our way along the side of the house.

Joe stopped behind a shrub. "Look! They're going back into the house! Let's move closer!"

We watched the two hooded figures enter the side door of the Rubins' house. Then we bolted across the street, our feet slipping on the wet lawn.

Sploosh!

I hit a puddle and—*whoomp*—my feet went out from under me. I landed on my back and slid across the grass. Joe tried to stop and help me. But then he lost his footing, too, and fell down next to me. As we scrambled to get up, we heard voices from the side of the house.

"They're coming back!" Joe whispered.

Rolling across the wet grass, we hid beneath a row of hedges. The two hooded men stepped out of the house carrying a large cardboard box. With a few grunts, they lifted it up and slid it into the van.

"What's up with this storm?" one of them shouted. "You were supposed to send data about a *fake* hurricane, not a *real* one."

"I *did!*" yelled the other. "This morning I hacked into the Weather Network's computer and sent them a false report. How was I supposed to know we'd get a little rain today?"

"A little rain? This is more like a typhoon!"

"Stop complaining. Everybody evacuated, didn't they? We can rob the whole town now."

"Yeah, but everything's getting wet!"

"Okay, crybaby. We'll take this load back to the warehouse and wait for the storm to pass."

The two men climbed into the front of the van. I tried to see their faces, but they slammed the doors before I could get a good look.

Vroooom!

The engine revved up with a loud roar. Exhaust fumes blew into our faces. Then the van started backing up out of the driveway.

"They're getting away!" yelled Joe.

Before I could stop him, he crawled out from the hedges and dashed across the yard.

"Joe! Wait!"

The van backed onto the street, then shifted

into drive. Joe ran up behind it—and climbed onto the rear bumper!

Are you crazy, Joe?

I scrambled to my feet and charged after him. He *was* crazy—but he wasn't doing this alone.

The van started pulling away. I sprinted into the street, running after the moving vehicle as it picked up speed.

I'm not going to make it.

The van zoomed faster down the street, moving farther away from me every second. But then it reached a corner and slowed down to make the turn. I surged forward, leaping and jumping onto the bumper.

I grabbed a handrail next to the sliding door and turned to look at Joe.

"Nice to see you could make it," he said.

"You're insane, Joe."

"I know you are, but what am I?" he replied.

He had a point. After all, there I was, right beside him, risking my life, riding on the back of a moving vehicle in the middle of a deadly storm.

Bracing my feet on the bumper, I pressed my body against the van and tightened my grip on the handrail.

Hold on, I told myself.

13.
Eye of the Storm

Man! I thought. *These guys drive like total maniacs!*

The moving van bobbed and bounced up and down, barreling through the streets of Bayport like a charging bull. I had to hold on with all my strength to keep from being catapulted off the back.

But the worst part was the weather.

Pounding sheets of rain assaulted us from every direction. The wind whistled and wailed and batted us around like a cat playing with a mouse. Water filled our eyes, ears, mouths, and nostrils, making it hard to see, hear, or even breathe.

Blinking away the rain, I glanced over at Frank.

He glared back at me, rolling his eyes and shaking his head.

Sorry, bro.

I knew he was angry with me for jumping onto the back of the van. But I *really* wanted to catch these guys—they were taking advantage of a crisis and deserved to go to jail.

That's what I told myself as the van hit a bump and nearly threw me to my death.

Hold on!

Water splashed up from the street. My feet slid across the wet bumper—and I slipped over the edge.

No!

With a swift jerk, my body dropped down and dangled over the road. My feet scraped against the pavement.

I'm a dead man.

Gripping the handrail with both hands, I pumped my arms and tried to pull myself up.

You can do it, I told myself.

Frank's eyes were wild and wet and filled with fear. Reaching out his hand, he tried to grab hold of me—but he was too far away.

You're on your own.

My fingers started to slip from the rail. I could feel myself losing my grip.

This is it, I thought. *You're going down.*

Suddenly the van lurched to one side and

rounded a corner. The sharp turn sent me reeling and swinging side to side until—

Yes, yes, yes!

My feet hit the bumper.

Scrambling to a standing position, I steadied myself against the back of the van and glanced over at Frank.

He stared back at me with a mixture of horror and relief.

Chill out, dude, I thought. *I'm still alive.*

I stuck out my tongue—and almost bit it off when the van hit another huge bump.

Frank and I bounced up in the air, our feet leaving the bumper and shooting backward.

WHAM!

Our bodies slammed back down again, smashing hard against the steel door of the van. After a little kicking and struggling, we managed to regain our footing. The van made another sharp turn, but this time we were ready for it.

Ka-thunk, ka-thunk!

The road beneath us suddenly got bumpier. I looked down and saw dirt and gravel instead of concrete.

We're close to the docks, I realized. *Finally.*

I turned my head and spotted the choppy waters of the bay. The storm was raging harder than ever now, and I couldn't make out the numbers of the warehouses as we drove by.

Are we there yet?

Suddenly the van screeched to a stop.

I looked at Frank. Without saying a word, we jumped off the bumper, dropped to the ground, and rolled underneath the van.

The two men opened the doors and got out.

"How long do you think this storm will last?"

"I don't know. Help me get this stuff inside."

They walked around to the back of the van. I could see their black rubber boots sink into the dirt just a few feet away from my face.

Who are you guys? I wondered for the millionth time.

They unlatched the metal door and slid it open. Then one of them grabbed a heavy object and dragged it toward the edge of the van.

"Grab the other end."

I heard a crackling electronic noise and a strange voice: *"Rescue 911, Rescue 911, please respond."*

It sounded like a walkie-talkie.

I glanced at Frank, who looked as puzzled as I was.

"Are you there? Rescue 911!"

I inched forward until I spotted a large walkie-

SUSPECT PROFILE

Name: Billy Wilson

Hometown: Bayport

Physical description: 19 years old, 5'8", 210 lbs.,
light brown hair, blue eyes, stocky build.

Occupation: Emergency rescue worker

Background: Got picked on as a scrawny kid, then
beefed up to play football and led Bayport High
School team to state victory, but was too short
to get a scholarship to play college football.

Suspicious behavior: "Rescued" Velma Carter, who
was later found poisoned, seen robbing the
Rubins' home and driving van of stolen goods.

Suspected of: Burglary, selling stolen property,
planting false weather reports, and murder.

Possible motive: Revenge against the town for
not receiving a football scholarship.

talkie dangling from a man's belt. A large hand
reached down, grabbed it, and pushed a red button.

"Yes, we read you."

The walkie-talkie crackled again. *"We've got a major hurricane situation here. Can you report to duty ASAP?"*

There was a short pause.

Then the man in front of me said, "Negative. We're handling another crisis right now."

I can't take this anymore, I thought. *I have to know who they are.*

Crawling in the mud a few inches closer, I ducked my head beneath the bumper to get a better look.

The man lowered the walkie-talkie and revealed his face. Then his partner leaned forward a little bit, and I was able to see him, too.

No way! It can't be them!

I blinked my eyes just to make sure it was true.

Yep, it's them.

I didn't want to believe it, but there they were: Wilson and Grady, the former football heroes from the Emergency Rescue Team!

I turned my head to look at Frank.

He seemed just as shocked as I was. But there wasn't much we could do about it right then and there. We were trapped beneath the van and half-buried in mud.

"Help me with this box, Greg," said Wilson.

Grady didn't move. "We're not going to re-spond to the 911 call?"

"No! We joined the team so we could *rob* people, not save them."

"Yeah, I know. But I feel bad about it—especially when it's a hurricane emergency."

"Shut up and help me move this stuff inside."

Grady stopped talking and helped his friend carry the box into the warehouse.

"Okay, the coast is clear," I said to Frank. "Let's go." I started to crawl out from under the van, but Frank grabbed me by the belt and pulled me back.

"Wait a minute," he said, reaching into his Windbreaker.

"What are you doing?"

"I want to check the weather again." He pulled out the emergency radio.

"Why?"

"Because I think this is a *real* hurricane."

Frank started playing with the knobs until he found a local weather report.

"After much confusion, weather authorities have confirmed that this *is* a hurricane," said the broadcaster. "Its name is *not* Jason, as reported by the Weather Network. This one is called Hurri-cane Joe, and the national experts say it could be

SUSPECT PROFILE

Name: Greg Grady

Hometown: Bayport

Physical description: 19 years old, 6'3", 240 lbs., dark hair, green eyes, large jaw, extremely muscular.

Occupation: Emergency rescue worker

Background: Grew up poor, played sports to become popular, named Bayport's Most Valuable Player, couldn't afford college—and couldn't get a scholarship due to bad grades.

Suspicious behavior: Seen robbing the Rubins' home with his high school friend Billy.

Suspected of: Burglary, selling stolen property, planting false weather reports, and murder.

Possible motive: Trying to raise money to pay for college.

the biggest storm ever to hit the Northeast coast."

Frank looked at me, then glanced nervously back at the warehouse.

"We believe it's a Category Four," the broadcaster continued. "So *please*—I urge you—if you evacuated your homes after the false reports of Hurricane Jason, *stay right where you are.* A very real storm is on its way. This is not a test. Hurricane Joe is coming."

I looked at Frank and shrugged. "So what if this is a real hurricane? We're here, and so are the burglars. Let's go get 'em."

Frank shook his head. "No way. We shouldn't even be here now. It's too dangerous. Just a few weeks ago, these docks were completely flooded. Remember?"

"What do *you* think we should do?"

"Go back to the evacuation center and tell Chief Collig about Wilson and Grady."

"But we're already here, Frank!"

"Yes, and we could die here too!"

The wind started howling even louder. The rain pounded down harder and heavier, forming huge puddles all around us. The sound of a steel door slamming made us look up.

"They're coming back," said Frank. "Stay down."

We watched Wilson and Grady running toward us through the rain.

Frank grabbed my arm. "Don't do anything stupid, Joe."

"Give me a break, Frank. What are you so afraid of?"

"Hurricane Joe is coming," he answered.

"Shhh."

Wilson and Grady jogged up to the truck and hopped into the back. We could hear them dragging things around and arguing back and forth.

I started to formulate a plan in my head.

We could launch a surprise attack: just grab their legs when they stepped out of the van and knock them to the ground.

But I figured Frank was right. We should forget about these guys and get away from the shore as quickly as possible.

Hurricane Joe is coming.

Wilson and Grady got out of the van. Their boots hit the ground with a soft thump—and splattered my face with mud.

I didn't do anything stupid.

But Frank did.

Believe it or not, he forgot to the turn the radio off.

With the loud wind and heavy rain, it shouldn't have a made a difference. Wilson and Grady would never have heard the broadcaster's voice under the van. But all of a sudden, without any warning, the rain stopped falling and the wind died down.

We were in the eye of the hurricane.

And all you could hear was a lone voice ringing out from the radio.

"HURRICANE JOE IS HERE."

For a second nobody moved. My brother and I held our breath. Wilson and Grady froze in their tracks. Even the puddles around us stopped rippling.

So much for my surprise attack.

Before the broadcaster could say another word, I grabbed the radio from Frank and turned it off.

"What was that?" said Wilson.

"I don't know."

"Did you leave the radio on inside the van?"

"No. It was probably one of the CD players we stole."

"Yeah, you're probably right."

I couldn't wait for the two guys to walk away. I was dying to let out a huge sigh of relief.

But for some strange reason, they didn't walk away. They just stood there outside the van, not talking or moving. I listened carefully, but all I could hear was the gentle lapping of the waves against the docks.

Then I thought I heard something: the sound of Wilson and Grady whispering.

But that didn't make any sense.

They think they're alone on the docks. Why would they whisper?

Then it hit me.

They know we're here.

I nudged Frank and pointed at the rescue workers' legs. I tried to hand-signal my plan for a surprise attack, but he didn't seem to understand.

It was too late anyway.

Wilson and Grady crouched down to the ground and poked their heads under the van.

"Hello, boys," Wilson said with a big, scary grin.

Then the two former football players grabbed us by the shoulders and dragged us kicking and screaming from our hiding place.

14.

Blown Away

"Hey! Let go!"

I swung my fists and pumped my legs, trying to break free from Wilson's grip. Joe rolled next to me in the mud. He didn't pull any punches either as he struggled to fight off Grady.

But let's face it—we didn't stand a chance.

Wilson and Grady were former football champs—and they had the strength, speed, and skill to prove it. Joe and I were like a pair of puppies compared to these bruisers.

Trying to fight them with our bare hands was a waste of time and energy.

"Take them into the warehouse," Wilson grunted to his buddy.

"What are we going to do to them?"

149

"What do you think?"

Great, I thought.

The last person who knew their identities ended up sipping a soda bottle full of poison.

This doesn't look good.

Grabbing us under the arms, they dragged us down the pier toward the warehouse door. Our feet and legs bounced and scraped against the wet wooden planks. It started raining again, but not very hard—just enough to blur our vision.

Clunk, clunk.

I felt myself being pulled over the threshold of the warehouse door. I blinked the rain out of my eyes and glanced up at Wilson.

"Put them in the corner," he barked.

Grady nodded and pulled Joe along by the neck of his Windbreaker.

WHUMP!

They tossed both of us into a heap on the floor. Then they stepped back and stood over us, glaring down at Joe and me like a pair of cobras getting ready to strike.

"I knew you brats were trouble," said Wilson. "As soon as I saw you at Velma's Pawnshop, I knew you were up to no good."

"Look who's talking," Joe shot back. "You creeps are the lowest of the low. Robbing people in the middle of a hurricane? It makes me sick."

Wilson lunged forward, pointing his finger in Joe's face. "You better watch your mouth, kid."

Joe wouldn't back off. "Or else what? You'll kill us?"

"We won't have to kill you," said Wilson. "The hurricane will take care of that."

I looked up. "What do you mean?"

"Yeah, Billy. What do you mean?" asked Grady.

Wilson crossed his arms over his chest and tapped his foot. "It's simple," he said. "Right now we're in the eye of the hurricane. But the storm is going to get worse. And when it does, you boys will take a nice long walk—down a very short pier."

Grady's eyes widened. "You mean . . . ?"

"Yep They're going to be victims of Hurricane Joe. Their bodies will be washed out to sea. And even if someone finds them on a beach somewhere, they'll never be able to trace it back to us."

I looked at Joe. He didn't look back—he just stared up at Wilson with total disgust.

"Okay, you got us, Wilson," I said. "But tell me how you did it. How did you get the Weather Network to report those fake hurricanes?"

A slow grin spread across Wilson's face. "It was easy. The Emergency Rescue Team has a computer that's linked directly into the Weather Network's mainframe. I made copies of old hurricane reports, changed some of the data, and made it look like it was sent from the national bureau's e-mail address."

I could tell he was proud of his scam.

"That's pretty darn clever," I said. "But why would a guy with computer skills turn to burglary? Why not go to school and get a job?"

The smile faded from Wilson's face. "I'll tell you why," he snapped. "This stupid little town refused to give us scholarships. Can you believe that? Grady and I won the state trophy for Bayport High, and what did we get in return? Nothing."

"We applied for college aid, but our grades weren't good enough," Grady added.

Wilson shot his buddy a dirty look. "That's none of their business, Greg."

"I just want them to know that we tried," said Grady. "We're not common criminals. We're saving money to go to school."

"Don't you get paid by the rescue team?" I asked.

"Yes, but not enough," said Grady.

Joe shook his head. "So you joined up just to rip people off?"

"Hey," Grady replied. "We saved people too."

"Like Velma Carter?" said Joe.

Grady gulped.

Wilson stomped his foot down. "Enough of this talk! Go find some rope so we can tie them up. They might try to make a run for it."

Grady turned around and lumbered off into the warehouse, leaving Joe and me alone with Billy Wilson.

It's two against one, I thought. *We have to do something while we have the chance.*

"You're not going to get away with this," Joe said, glaring up at Wilson.

"Oh, no? Why not?"

Joe started telling him a whopper of a lie—that the police found their names in Velma's Pawnshop records and they were already on their way—but I didn't pay much attention.

I was too busy looking around for a weapon.

I leaned back against a wooden crate and gazed upward. Sticking out over the edge was a large silver serving tray—the kind you would use for a fancy tea party.

Perfect.

"I got the rope!" Grady yelled from across the warehouse.

Wilson leaned over Joe and snarled, "You're lying, kid. The police aren't coming."

Grady started walking toward us.

I had to move fast.

Reaching up, I grabbed the silver tray with both hands.

It's teatime.

I swung it through the air as hard as I could—and slammed Wilson in the side of the head.

CLANG!

"Ooof!"

Wilson went down like a ton of bricks.

You've been served.

Unfortunately, he landed right on top of Joe, who wriggled beneath the ex-football player like a squashed bug. Finally he managed to crawl out from under him and jump to his feet.

Wilson was stunned and dazed—but reviving fast.

I reached into the crate, pulled out a teapot, and tossed it to my brother.

"Thanks, bro."

Joe tightened his grip on the handle—and offered Wilson another serving.

CLANG!

"Ooof!"

Down he went.

I would have cheered, but I had another problem to contend with: Greg Grady was hunched down and charging straight toward me. In about three seconds, I was going to be tackled by a 240-pound former linebacker.

This is going to hurt.

But it was Grady who got hurt—because I used the serving tray as a shield. A split second before he hit me, I slipped it over my chest and braced myself.

CLANG!

Greg Grady smashed face-first into the tray and stumbled to the ground, banging his knee into a wooden crate.

"Owww! My bad knee!" he howled, writhing on the floor.

I looked at Joe. "Let's get out of here!"

We ran to the door of the warehouse. Reaching up, we grabbed the steel bolt and pushed hard.

Nothing happened. The door wouldn't open.

"It's locked," said Joe. "What'll we do?"

I tried to think.

Suddenly, without warning, the whole warehouse started to shake. The floorboards creaked and groaned. The wind lashed at the walls and the rain pounded the roof like a big bass drum. I could even hear the waves crashing against the pier, pummeling the sides of the building.

"The window," said Joe, pointing. "Upstairs."

We ran for the stairs.

"Hurry!"

I glanced over my shoulder. Wilson and Grady were climbing to their feet—and coming after us.

"You can run, but you can't hide!" Wilson shouted.

He and his buddy charged up the stairs.

"You're trapped!"

Joe and I scrambled up to the balcony and turned around. Then we grabbed whatever we could find—TV sets, computers, Zboxes—and started throwing them down the stairs.

"Ouch! My knee!"

Grady stumbled down the stairs. But Wilson jumped out of the way, knocking the items aside with his hands and feet. Grady picked himself up and joined Wilson on the stairs. Working as a team, they managed to toss the heavy computers and TVs over the railing like they were baby toys. Then they rushed up the stairs.

These guys are unstoppable.

I looked around for something else to throw— and that's when Wilson grabbed me by the arm.

"Gotcha!" he growled.

Running to my aid, Joe tried to tackle Wilson. But—

WHAM!

Grady tackled Joe first.

The two of them slammed down hard on the floor of the balcony. Rolling around, they kicked and fought until—*bang*—Joe hit his head against a wooden crate.

His eyelids fluttered and closed—and then his whole body went limp.

"Joe! No!"

I screamed and tried to pull away from Wilson. But he held on to me with both hands, dragging me toward the steel shelves against the wall.

"Put the kid inside one of those crates," he said to Grady.

The former linebacker grunted and picked up Joe with one arm. Then he dumped my brother into an empty crate and sat down on the lid.

"Joe! Wake up! Joe!"

Wilson laughed. "Don't waste your breath. You'll need it when you're underwater."

I stopped struggling. He stared at me and smiled. Then he shoved me against the shelving unit, pressing my arms against the cross braces.

"Greg, where did you put that rope?" he shouted over his shoulder.

"It's downstairs."

"Go and get it."

"But what about . . . ?" Grady pointed at the crate he was sitting on.

"The kid is out like a light. Just put something heavy on it."

Grady got up and moved a giant forty-eight-inch TV onto the lid of the crate. Then he turned and ran down the stairs.

Wilson looked at me but didn't say anything.

Outside the warehouse, the hurricane raged on—even stronger and fiercer than before. Rain pounded on the roof so hard I was afraid it would cave in. A giant wave crashed against the side of the building and shook it from top to bottom.

Even Wilson had to flinch.

"Scared, Wilson?" I said.

He glared at me. I raised my chin and held his gaze. But out of the corner of my eye, I saw the lid of the crate slowly rise.

It's Joe. He's okay.

"Of course I'm not scared," Wilson snarled.

"Really?" I said calmly. "You should be."

He scoffed. "Why?"

"Hurricane Joe is here," I said.

WHUMP!

The giant TV set crashed to the floor.

Joe jumped out of the crate—and leaped onto Wilson's back.

THUMP!

They hit the floor and rolled. I grabbed a ceramic

vase off the shelf behind me and smashed it over Wilson's head.

CRASH!

He slumped to the floor. I reached for Joe's arm and pulled him to his feet. "Let's go! Through the window!"

We turned and started climbing the shelving unit like a giant ladder, scrambling up as fast as we could. Halfway to the top, I felt the rain lashing down from the open window above us. Just a few more feet and—

Someone grabbed my ankle.

I looked down. It was Grady, climbing up after us. Right behind him was Wilson, grasping a shelf with one hand and reaching for Joe with the other.

"Joe! Look out!"

Wilson's hand wrapped around Joe's ankle and started pulling him down.

Another wave crashed against the side of the building. The beams inside cracked and split. The ceiling buckled. The wind howled like some sort of wild animal caught in a trap.

And then something happened that none of us could ever have imagined.

The wind ripped the roof off.

JOE

15.
Hurricane Joe

With a single deafening roar, the whole roof was wrenched right off the top of the building—exposing us to the killer wind and rain of Hurricane Joe.

I couldn't believe my eyes.

One second the roof was just a few feet above our heads, protecting us from a full-blown hurricane. The next second it was gone.

Gone!

Totally blown away!

Nobody spoke. Nobody screamed.

The four of us were in shock.

Wilson, Grady, Frank, and I clung to the shelving unit, staring wide-eyed at the stormy sky. Another huge wave crashed against the building and flooded the lower floor.

Then the water started rising.

I'm sure all of us were thinking the same thing.

What a way to die.

But then I realized I had to do something if I wanted to survive. I scrambled to the top of the shelving unit and grabbed Frank's arm. Pulling him up, I pointed to the window.

"You first!" he shouted over the howling wind.

I glanced down at Wilson and Grady.

They were still clinging to the shelves, staring down in disbelief. Another wave surged through the warehouse, ripping through another wall.

"Go, Joe! Don't look back!"

Frank shoved me through the window.

"Frank! Wait!" I shouted back at him.

"What?"

"The pier! It's gone!"

I gazed down at the churning water below the window. The docks were completely flooded.

Frank poked his head out to see for himself.

"What should we do?" I shouted.

"Jump!" he yelled back.

"But Frank—"

"We can't stay here! We'll be crushed!"

Suddenly the warehouse shifted and swayed.

Beams and floorboards cracked and broke apart. Then a massive gust of wind started tearing the whole building apart.

"Jump, Joe! Jump!"

I jumped.

Splash!

I hit the water hard, plunging down, deep beneath the waves. For a second I was afraid I was going to drown. But then I remembered the ultra-slim life vest underneath my Windbreaker.

Groping for the pull-string, I gave it a hard tug.

Whoosh!

The vest filled up with air—and carried me to the surface. My head popped out of the water. Gasping for air, I started swimming for the shore.

"Joe! Help me!"

I turned my head and spotted Frank about twenty feet away. He was bobbing up and down in the waves—and having a hard time staying afloat.

"Your life vest!" I yelled. "Use your life vest!"

My brother dipped down and disappeared.

Frank? Frank!

I started to panic. But then I saw my brother shoot up out of the water, his life vest filled with air. He waved his arm and started swimming toward me.

CRRRRRUUUUNCH!

A loud—and terrifying—sound made us both turn around and look.

It was the warehouse.

The storm tore a huge hole right through the middle of it, slamming the building like a sledge-hammer and sending pieces of wood and debris splashing in all directions.

Then, with another loud crunch, the warehouse collapsed—and disappeared into the water.

I looked back at Frank. "There's no way Wilson and Grady survived that."

My brother sighed long and hard. Then he nodded to something behind me. I turned and saw a bunch of wooden crates floating toward us.

"Grab onto one!"

We started swimming toward them, but it was hard to make any headway with the strong current. Finally we each managed to reach the crates. Clinging onto the sides, we kicked our legs and tried to set a course toward the shore.

After a while, the rain started slowing down, and so did we.

"Frank! I'm getting tired!"

"Hang in there!"

"Are we going the right way?"

"I sure hope so!"

I have to admit: I was getting a little worried.

The tides were rising, and I couldn't even see the shoreline through all the rain.

Suddenly I spotted something.

"Frank! Look!"

I pointed to a pair of flashing lights coming toward us through the mist.

"It's a rescue boat!" I shouted. "We're saved!"

We waited for the boat to get a little closer. Then we started yelling and waving our arms in the air.

"Help! Help! HELP!!!"

The rescue boat slowed down and veered toward us.

Yes!

A couple of rescuers pulled up beside us. "We got you, boys," said a tall, balding man. "Just give me your hand."

He and his partner reached down and pulled Frank and me out of the water and into the boat. We stumbled on board and started to thank our rescuers.

But then we noticed that we weren't the only ones they had rescued.

No. It can't be.

Wilson and Grady sat in the back of the boat, dripping wet and shivering.

"Hello, boys," said Wilson, with a smirk.

The tall rescuer introduced us. "That's Wilson and Grady," he said to us. "They're members of our team."

I started shaking my head. "They're criminals, that's what they are."

The tall man looked at me like I was crazy. "What are you talking about?"

"Those are the guys who are behind all of the burglaries," I said. "They faked the hurricanes so people would evacuate their houses."

Wilson scoffed. "He's lying. The kid's delirious from being in the water so long."

The tall man looked into my eyes. "You must be mistaken, young man. Wilson and Grady are emergency rescuers. I've worked with them for over a year now."

The other man turned and said, "I think you boys should sit down and relax." He nodded toward the seats next to Wilson and Grady.

Frank and I sighed and sat down.

What choice did we have? The rescuers refused to believe that their coworkers were crooks.

Wilson and Grady didn't even look at us. They just sat there while the other rescuers went back to work, manning the controls and searching the water for survivors.

Then they made their move.

Wilson grabbed Frank by the throat. Grady did the same to me. Standing up, they pushed us backward until we were hanging over the side of the boat.

Then they shoved us downward, lower and lower. Water splashed over our faces.

They're going to kill us!

Suddenly I felt something wrench Grady away from me. Another hand pulled me up as I gasped for air. I opened my eyes to see the tall man grabbing Wilson by the shoulders. With a strong jerk, he threw him off of Frank and helped my brother into the boat.

The two rescuers shoved Wilson and Grady to the floor.

"So the kid was right," said the tall man. "You're criminals, aren't you?"

Wilson and Grady glared back without saying a word.

"No answer, huh?" The tall rescuer shook his head. "That's okay. You have the right to remain silent."

Then he turned the boat around and headed back to Bayport.

Hurricane Joe didn't last very long. By the following morning it had changed direction and drifted off into the ocean. By the following afternoon it was nothing more than a mid-Atlantic breeze.

But it sure left a lot of devastation in its wake—and most of it seemed to be right in our own front yard.

"Stack up those branches next to the garage," Aunt Trudy ordered us. "All the other debris can go into these garbage bags."

I leaned against the porch railing and sighed. "Can't this wait until tomorrow, Aunt Trudy? Frank and I are totally bushed."

She shook her head. "No, it's a mess out here. And speaking of bushes, you can dig up that old rosebush in the corner. It's utterly destroyed."

"I'm utterly destroyed," I muttered to Frank. "Can't you think of a way to distract her? You're supposed to be the smart one."

Frank wrinkled his brow. A second later his eyes lit up. "Aunt Trudy!" he said. "Come here!"

She walked across the porch and stopped in front of us. "Yes? What is it?"

"You never told us why nobody calls you Gertrude."

"I don't *let* them call me Gertrude," she replied.

"Why not?" asked Frank. "It's your real name, isn't it?"

She nodded and sat down on the porch bench.

"It happened years ago. I was born with the name Gertrude, and that's what everyone called me. I thought it was such a lovely name. But then one day . . ."

She paused.

"What?" I asked.

"Hurricane Gertrude destroyed half of Bayport," she answered.

"Wow! A hurricane? With the same name?" I said.

Aunt Trudy smiled. "Everyone started calling me Hurricane Gertrude. Everywhere I went, people would say, 'Hello, Hurricane Gertrude,' and 'Nice weather we're having, Hurricane Gertrude.' It drove me crazy."

"That's understandable," I said. "Who wants to share a name with a disaster?" I wasn't having such a hard time brushing off the whole Hurricane Joe thing—but maybe that was because of the way the storm ended. Calm skies.

"Nobody, Joe. That's why I changed my name. From that moment on, I insisted that people call me Trudy. End of story."

She snapped her fingers and stood up. "Now, get back to work."

"But Aunt Trudy—"

"No buts," she said, holding up a finger. "I've

been cleaning up after Hurricane Joe *and* Hurricane Frank for years now. It's time you boys returned the favor."

She walked to the doorway.

"And don't forget to fix the mailbox."

Then she was gone.

I sighed and picked up a rake. "You know what, Frank? We get no respect. We manage to catch Bayport's most wanted criminals, and what's our reward?"

"The satisfaction of making the world a better place?" he said with a smile.

"No, our reward is *this*." I pointed at the lawn. "We have to clean up this—this mud puddle, also known as our front yard."

"That's the price of being an undercover agent, Joe. No one knows what a hero you are."

"Well, I wish I was known for *something*."

Just then Chet Morton rode by on his bike.

"Yo! Hurricane Joe!" he shouted.

I looked at Frank and sighed.

"Hey, if it doesn't work for you, you can always change your name to Joseph," he said. "Or *Josephine*."

I jabbed him in the ribs and got back to work. "I'll stick with Joe, thanks."